ADDICTED TO A DIRTY SOUTH 4

SHAN

MYSS SHAN

SUBSCRIBE

Text Shan to 22828 to stay up to date with new releases, sneak peeks, contest, and more...
Or sign up Here
Check your spam if you don't receive an email thanking you for signing up.

PREVIOUSLY

Last time in Addicted to a Dirty South Thug 3....

Cuba

I got the text from Khi asking me what the medicine was that, I guess, he found wherever my ass couldn't find it. I thought that I had looked everywhere possible. Shit had been so crazy that it slipped my mind to even go back for it, and I had completely forgotten about it up until now.

Shit, fuck it and fuck him, I thought, as I tossed the phone into the passenger's seat. I did what I felt I had to do for my own sanity, and that was to get rid of my damn child. All I did was worry about whether or not it was gonna come out all fucked up or something because of that shit that Briana had pumped into me.

I know what the doctor said, and I was well aware that they were running test on me, but who's to say that it would've been one hundred percent.

I just didn't wanna take that chance and bring a baby into this world that was always sick and suffering because of something that had nothing to do with it. It didn't matter what Khi thought though now, because I was leaving him, and this time, I promised myself that I wasn't gonna go back.

I couldn't believe that he cheated on me with that hoe Selena. The day that Briana blurted it out when me, her, and Selena were all together, and when she kept fucking with me, that bitch really was telling the truth. Khi had fucked Selena...but damn, why'd he have to get her pregnant?

It was so fucked up, because I had gone back and forth so many times about whether what I was doing was right when it came time to use those pills, and a few times, I had talked myself out of it. My thoughts got the best of me eventually, and they drove me wild. Every time I would close my damn eyes, I would see that bitch Briana stabbing me with that needle. At night when I was able to sleep, I would dream that my child came out addicted to heroin and struggling to breathe. It was like everything was pushing me to do it, and the day that Khi got locked up, I felt like it was best, so I made the decision.

Most times I felt right about it, but times like this, I felt like God was punishing me for what I had done. Selena was gonna get to give Khi his first son—the son that I was supposed to give him. Man, he doesn't know how bad that hurts.

I shook my head as more tears fell down my face, but I quickly wiped them away and tried my best to focus on the road. It had just started to pour down and with my window being broken, and all the crying I had been doing, it was becoming hard to see.

I turned my right signal on and got ready to get off at the next exit, but my car hit what felt like a huge hole in the road and caused my wheel to shake uncontrollably. I tried to steady it, but the front tires seemed to lock up and forced me to swerve off the road. I slammed down on the brakes just in time.

"Oh, fuck!" I yelled out when I tried to back up but the tires seemed to be still locked up. I punched my hand into the steering wheel and took my seatbelt off. It was raining hard as hell, but I needed to get out to see if I would be able to see what was going on.

I pushed the door open quickly, stepped out, and didn't notice anything wrong. When I walked around to the other side, I instantly noticed that my front tire was bent and damn near hanging off. I frowned and shook my head confused as to how that could even happen after hitting a damn pothole.

Walking back around to the driver's side, I got back in the car and closed the door behind me. I went to pick up my cell phone that sat in the passenger's seat when I could hear someone pulling in behind me. Looking through the rearview mirror, I could tell by the sign on the front that it was Tahoe. I decided to send Tangie a text to let her know what happened and not to worry about me.

Me: Ran over a pothole and my car all fucked up. About to call Roadside assistance. Be there soon.

Send.

Just as I was about to make the call to roadside assistance, there was a shadow standing over my car. I looked up and the guy looked oddly familiar. Even through the rain that fell onto his face and in mine, I could see that I had known him from somewhere.

"Hi," I told him.

"Yuh need some help?" he asked me and I shook my head. He had a deep accent sounding as if he was from the islands or somewhere nearby them.

"No, I'm about to call roadside. My rim is all fucked up, so I think I need a tow."

"Yuh should make that call from my truck. It's not safe for yuh to be sitting on the side of the road like tis. Let me take yuh to a car service place, and we can tell them where yuh car is."

"No, that's okay. I'm okay," I told him with a smile.

"Yuh the pretty girl that I saw trying on the dress that day. Did yuh walk down the aisle yet?" he asked me, and I tossed my head back now realizing where I had seen him at. He was the sexy ass nigga that was a built like a damn God and staring me down the day I was trying on wedding gowns. The only difference between then and now was that he didn't have any dreads.

"Oh, my God, I'm so embarrassed for the way I was looking at you that day."

"Don't be. Come on, let me take yuh. I got mi little brother with me, and we were just headed to get something to eat. I don't mind at all."

"I looked through the rearview mirror and then up at him. Shit, it was raining hard as hell, and I was stuck in the middle of the highway. I knew that, if I sat here and waited for a tow truck to come, I would be waiting for at least an hour, and by then I would be soaked in water and sick as hell by morning.

"Okay...let me just grab my purse," I told him and grabbed my bag from the passenger's seat. I took the keys out of the ignition and tossed them into my purse before I got out the car and ran behind him to his truck. He opened the back door for me, and I hopped inside.

The moment he closed the door, I reached for my seatbelt to put it on, and that was when I raised my head to see who was sitting in the front seat. I had never met him in person and had only seen pictures of him around my house.

"Cuba, this is my little brother Emon. Emon, this is Khi's wife, Cuba," the guy said and laughed as he turned around and violently snatched my cell phone and purse from my hand.

Shit; I thought to myself on what to do next. This nigga knew my name, who my husband was, and had Emon tied up in the front seat of the car. I guess this was why Khi said never leave home without him or any of his goonies. I had evaded our old home with hopes to get away from him and his whack ass security, and I did just that only to find myself into some trouble that I wasn't sure I was gonna be able to get out of.

The fuck am I gonna do now?

1

CUBA

"Aghhhhhh! Get off of me! Get the fuck off of me!" I yelled, as Chaison rubbed his hands up and down my thighs while keeping my arms pinned to the bed above me. "Please... don't...please!"

"Yuh got a pretty ass pussy, gal. Wet, too. Tell meh I don't turn yuh on. I saw how yuh look at meh at the wedding place," Chaison said, as he looked down at me. I closed my eyes and bit down hard on my bottom lip when Chaison's lips grazed across my skin. The moment he pushed my legs open, I began to scream at the top of my lungs and wiggled around as best as I could.

"Oh God...please, noooo," I cried out, when I felt his erection centered at the opening of my vagina.

"Szzzz, so wet," Chaison groaned before licking his tongue around my ear.

"No...no...donnnn'tttttt!"

BAM! BAM! BAM!

DING-DONG! DING-DONG! DING-DONG!

"Shit!" I hissed, as I sat up in bed and looked around the room. I glanced over at the digital clock on my nightstand and sighed seeing that it was only three in the morning. I couldn't believe that I was having that same damn dream again. Seemed like, no matter how many times I tried to block those events out of my life, I was always haunted with the memory of it in my sleep.

BAM! BAM! BAM!

I damn near jumped out of my skin and looked around for my cell phone when I found it in between the nightstand and the bed. I snatched it up from the floor and noticed that I had tons of missed calls and messages. Rolling my eyes, I made my way to the front door, peeped out of the hole, and then pulled the door open.

"So you just sitting there ignoring my damn calls," Khi said and frowned, as I crossed my arms over my chest. He grabbed my hand and looked at it before he pushed past me and walked inside of my home.

"I told you not to ever let him up here without asking me first," I said to one of the security guards that Khi had securing the house. Khi and I had been split up since the last fight we had in the driveway of his old house over his baby mama Selena. Come to find out, the baby wasn't even his, but still, knowing that he had slept with her, hid her pregnancy from me, and seemed to have no plans of ever telling me was enough for me to call everything off with him. Not to mention, getting caught up in his bullshit with Chaison, and the horror I had to go through with that situation, it just had me completely over everything.

Khi begged and begged while constantly sending me gifts like he always had thinking that was gonna get me to change my mind, but I was done. I loved that man so much and hated him in the same breath. He was the cause of my happiest moments and the reason for my darkest days. I knew that he loved me, but he didn't respect me, and because of that, no amount of love would ever be enough.

"I pay that nigga's salary and for this muthafuckin' house," Khi said, and I scoffed as I slammed the door and turned to look at him.

"By choice. Don't act like I asked you to."

"Fuck is your ring at?" he asked, and out of curiosity, I scanned his hand for his. When I spotted it, I placed my hands behind my back and cocked my head to side while staring him up and down.

"Khi, you came here to cuss me out. What do you want? I was sleep, and I have to get up and go to work in the morning."

"Where's your ring at, Cuba?" Khi asked, and I could sense the sadness in his voice. I shook my head and sighed. I had to look away from him. I hated when he made me feel bad about the decisions I made when it came to our relationship—our marriage. I loved him—but he hurt me. I was still in love with him, but I couldn't help but wonder if he made me his wife because he felt like it would make me stay after the truth was revealed. And the love I had for him wasn't nearly enough to make me forget about Chaison.

Oh, my God, I thought to myself as I ran my hand down the side of my leg and bit down on my lip to keep from crying.

"Had some...some stuff I did at client's house that got messy, and I didn't want it to get dirty," I lied.

Khi nodded and looked around the house before turning his attention back to me; he slowly came towards me. I swallowed back hard and became more and more nervous the closer he had gotten.

"Is everything okay?" I asked and cleared my throat before taking two steps back. Khi came closer, and I backed up some more until my back was against the wall and I had no room left to move. My gaze went to the floor, and this moment reminded me of the times when my heart would flutter any time Khi got this close to me...the sad thing was, nothing had changed.

"Baby, please tell me what I gotta do to have you back in my life. Cuba, why the fuck you doing me like this? Nigga ain't been right since," Khi said, causing a tear to fall from my eye. I quickly brought my hand up to wipe it away when Khi placed a finger under my chin and forced me to look up at him. My lip quivered, and I refused to make eye contact with him. I knew that it was tearing him up based off of his appearance, and the fact that every time I saw him, he was either drunk, high, leaning, or all of the above. He no longer wore suit and ties and had even let his facial hair grow out to a lengthy beard.

I felt bad, but I didn't. Because of Khi, I had suffered at the hands of Brianna, had to find out from his other baby mama that he had cheated, and then Chaison...

"Khi, I'm...I'm not in love with you anymore. Why do you keep doing this?" I said as I sniffled.

"Baby..."

"Khi, no! I told you. You promised me if I took this house from you that you would leave me alone. I don't wanna be with you anymore. Just give me a divorce and let me move on with my life."

"Cuba, you never even gave me a chance to fuckin' explain! I forgave your ass when you killed my muthafuckin' seed!" Khi roared after slamming his fist into the door behind me.

I screamed out and kneeled down in fear that he would hit me. That was another reason why I just had to let it go, and why I didn't want his ass coming to my house. With each day that went by that I told this man no, and that I was done, his attitude and disrespect towards me grew. He hadn't put his hands on me, but I felt like one day it was coming.

"Khi, get away from me! Get out! Now...go!" I yelled at him as I stayed low and closer to the ground. He reached out for me, and I squealed out in fear, causing Khi to step back and take a deep breath. I looked up at him and hurried to open the front door. I saw now that I was gonna have to get my own fuckin' place and not even tell Khi where I had moved to. It seemed like it was the only way I was going to get peace and get over the heartache I felt.

"Tangie... she's in labor. I told her I would come and get you and bring you the hospital," Khi told me, and I exhaled before closing the door back.

"O...ok. Let me put on some clothes, and I'll be right back."

I stepped forward and had to walk around Khi to get to my room being that he refused to move out of my way. He was always using any excuse that he could to get over it and fuck with me. One day, it would be because Skylarr wanted to see me, even though he was doing his all to keep her from me when I decided to leave. The next, it would be because he needed me to sign some documents on a bank account he opened or other petty shit.

I couldn't fault the man for trying, but it was over, and I wish he had just left well enough alone. He was making me feel so bad when I knew that the decision I was making was the right one. Staying with a nigga after all this shit would only make him think I was some weak ass bitch that he could walk over anytime he felt like it. A couple of fuck-ups and some makeups were cool, but I could no longer be the fool. It hurt, but it wouldn't always.

I went into my bedroom and walked over to the dresser where I kept some of my clothing. I pulled out a bra, a wife beater, and a pair of Pink sweat pants before pulling off the satin nightgown I was wearing. As soon as I snapped my bra together, and pulled it around to the front of my body, I could feel Khi's presence in my room. He had gotten me so flustered and nervous that I had completely forgotten to close and lock my damn door.

"That nigga did this to you?" Khi asked, and I quickly turned around and grabbed my shirt, trying to put it on, but Khi stopped me.

"Let me go!" I screamed and jerked my arm away from him.

"I thought you told me nothing happened, Cuba!"

"Just take me to the hospital to see Tangie. Nothing happened that matters. Get the hell out of my room so I can put my clothes on," I spewed angrily and tried to shake away the tears that were threatening to fall.

"You blame me for that shit, huh? That's why you won't talk to me and treat me so bad when you do see me? I guess if I had never fucked Selena, then you would've never ran off, and that nigga Chaison would have never gotten his hands on you. What he do to you?"

"Like I said, nothing that matters," I told Khi as I slid my sweats on and glided my feet into the flip-flops that sat next to my bed.

"Does Emon know what happened? He seems to get a little attitude too whenever I bring the shit up?"

"Maybe you should stop bringing it up then. I'm ready."

I brushed past Khi and headed out of my bedroom and out of the house. What happened during that whole ordeal with Chaison, me, and Emon was nothing I wanted to relive. I would never talk about it, and as soon as I could stop having fucked up ass dreams about what happened, I would never think about it again either. Fuck Chaison... and fuck Khi.

2

TANGIE

"Ughhhh! I think he's too big for me to push out!" I screamed and then fell back onto the back of the bed. I closed my eyes becoming more and more frustrated with this whole process. I was only eight months along and had gone into labor unexpectedly in the middle of the night after my water had broken. I thought that I had time like I had seen on many movies where a woman's water would break and they walked around laughing, eating, and doing all kind of shit before finally going to the hospital, so I had text Cass to let him know what was up, took a shower, and fixed me a sandwich before excruciating pain came out of nowhere.

Cass was across town, more than forty minutes away, supposedly handling business, so I had gotten Emon to drive me to the hospital. By the time I had gotten here, and into a gown, I found out that I was nine centimeters along and too far gone for me to get an epidural.

"I can give you thirty more minutes, but after that, we're gonna have to go another route," my doctor, Doctor Sandoval told me, and I tried my best to keep my cool. I looked over at the clock and saw that it was almost 4:30 in the morning, and that I had been here pushing for almost two hours, but had yet to produce my unborn son.

Dr. Sandoval explained to me that sometimes babies had a hard time passing through the birth canal with women who had small frames and that either suctioning or getting a C-Section was the only alternative. I didn't want neither.

"Has he called yet?" I asked the nurse that stood on the side of me holding my hand.

"Not yet. I was told that your cousin and brother-in-law are on the way though," she answered, and before I could even allow a tear to fall, I felt another contraction coming, which meant it was time for me to push again. I couldn't believe I was doing this shit alone. Cass was supposed to be there. He had even text me to say that he was on his way, but that was over two damn hours ago, and I hadn't heard a word from him.

I had Emon get in contact with Khi after not being able to reach Cuba, because I just wanted someone there, so I didn't have to do it alone, but now I was exhausted and tired of the pain.

"Aagghhhhhh!" I screamed after pushing as hard and as long as I possibly could. "I can't...I can't. Please, let's just do the C-Section."

"It's okay. It's not your fault. Sometimes this happens," my doctor ensured me, but it didn't stop me from feeling like a failure. I looked towards the door just as it came open, and that quickly, the sorrow I felt turned into a little bit of happiness upon seeing Cuba walk in. She rushed to my side and kissed me on my forehead.

"I can't push him out. His father isn't here," I cried, and Cuba grabbed my hand and kissed the back of it.

"It's okay. I'm here. You know I got you, cuz. Don't even worry about a thing."

"Is he okay?"

"He's...he's not gonna make it," Cuba told me, and I just broke down, furious, hurt, and just fucking tired of every damn thing.

"We gotta go now, Ms. Lance. I'm sorry, but we don't have a lot of time," the nurse explained to me, and I nodded.

～

"What's wrong? Is he okay, Cuba?" I asked again while the medical team prepped to roll me out of the room.

"I don't know what happened. On the way here, Khi got a call that he was arrested on murder charges. Khi dropped me off and went to go see about him. Don't worry, though, Tangie. Just get my little cousin into this world safely, and everything is gonna be good."

I could barely hear anything that Cuba was saying to me. The moment the words arrested on murder charges had left her mouth, everything else around me seemed to go in slow motion. Cass just couldn't seem to stay out of trouble. It was always something with him. Like, he just had the worst fuckin' luck at the worst fuckin' time.

I had given him another chance, and we attended counseling for about six weeks, and things were good between us. I had found out a lot about Cass... some things that I had never known, and he had even found out some things about me. We were on the right track, and I had even stepped up to be a mother to his daughter Cassie after Jourdin, for some reason, ran off the night Cass went to pick up his phone that he'd left.

It had been three months, and she had yet to come back or even call to check on her child. It was fine with me, though, because Cassie was a beautiful and sweet little girl. She did everything I asked of her, and it was only times when she would long for her mother that I would have any issues out of her, but it was all understandable.

It was just crazy how Jourdin could walk away from her child like that. I had only known the little girl for a short amount of time and couldn't imagine never seeing or talking to her again. She was such an angel with her funny looking eyes that were exactly like her father's.

At first, I was somewhat jealous that Jourdin had given Cassidy a child when I had lost mine, but the further I had gotten into my pregnancy, the less any of that even mattered anymore. I was getting ready to bring his first son into this world, and what was supposed to be a glorious occasion was turning into a fuckin' nightmare. Seemed like Cass was never here for me when I needed him. This shit was reminding me of the last time, when I had to push out my dead child with Khi here, instead of the person that had gotten me pregnant, because he had gotten locked up.

"Don't cry, Tangie; it's gonna be okay," Cuba said to me breaking me from the deep trance-like state that I had fallen into.

"It's not gonna be okay, Cuba...argghhhhh!" I gritted down as another contraction hit me tearing through my back and then to my stomach. I gripped a hold of Cuba's hand and closed my eyes tightly waiting on the pain to somewhat subside.

"The operating room is ready now, Ms. Lance; we'll take you down to get prepped," my nurse told me, and I could only nod my head.

"Oh, my God. I don't know if I wanna have a baby now," Cuba joked, and I tried to laugh, but everything was just so wrong. I was about to be a mother to my own kid finally.... something that I had always wanted, but a single mother? This was not supposed to be my life.

Fuck! Why was I always letting this nigga get me caught up? Fuck him. I'm done.

3

KAEDEE

"Get the fuck out my face," I yelled at Destiny, as she kneeled in front of me begging me to forgive her.

"KaeDee, please, you gotta listen to me. I promise you it's not what it seems like," Destiny cried, and I scoffed, quickly sliding my hands into my pockets.

"What the hell you mean it's not what it seems like? Your fuckin' partner called my brother month's ago and told him what you had been up to, and my dumb ass didn't wanna believe him or her. You better be so fuckin' glad that you carrying my damn child right now; I would murder your police ass!"

"Do you really think your life would be so much better with that bitch Deonna around? She was a fraud that connived her way through life, and it would've been only a matter of time before her shit took you and your brothers down. I saved you...I saved all of y'all!"

"Didn't need you to fuckin' save me by sending that nigga Tyrin after my wife. You set all that shit up. The new charges against them, him knowing where my office was, and where the fuck me and my family rested our heads! You ain't got no room to say shit about her, because you just as conniving! Get the fuck up and bounce Destiny, before I have you dragged from my property!" I roared and had to step back to keep myself from snapping on her.

I hated when I lost my cool, because it took everything to calm me down. This shit with Destiny though was just beyond my wildest damn nightmares. This chick had come through and had changed my life for, what I thought at first, the better. She knew that everything for me was purely physically, and that I was still mourning and hurt behind Deonna. I didn't have no type of feelings for Destiny, but she was persistent. She rode for me through it all, helped me through my darkest days, and made sure I got to the point where I could function like the man I used to be.

Destiny became my backbone, taking care of me and the kid without ever complaining. She had risked her job and her life more times than she should have just to prove to me and my brothers that her badge didn't mean shit. After all that, the love came along with it. I felt like she was a rider...like how I had once felt about Deonna.

Even when Khi came to me to tell me about all the things that Destiny's partner was saying about her some months back, I wasn't even trying to hear any of it, because to me, she had proven herself. Not only that, Destiny had already informed me that her partner was jealous and had done a lot of dirty shit towards here.

She had me convinced that everything her partner was accusing her of was shit she had done herself but was trying to place the blame on Destiny. As of late, some things had come into play that made me question whether or not she had been lying to me.

I started having her followed and investigated about a month ago, and the bitch was worse than Deonna.

At least with Deonna, I had always felt like, he who finds a wife, finds a good thing, so whatever she did was forgivable. Destiny, on the other hand, had taken it upon herself to get rid of my wife as if I needed her to. She had those charges filed against Tyrin and Deonna, sparking up everything that had led to her murder.

No matter what she said, she was just as guilty as the nigga that had pulled the trigger. She was lucky that she was carrying my damn child or else I would've taken her the fuck out. Grimy ass bitch.

"So this is it? You just gonna put me out on my ass with no place to go while I'm carrying your child, KaeDee," Destiny sneered, and I got sick to my stomach looking at her. She was now the woman that had taken my child's mother away from her. The sight of her was one I didn't think I could ever stand again.

"You'll be straight. You got your peoples that live not too far from here. Hit em up and let em know you ain't shit and tell em to keep your muthafuckin' ass away from me before I hurt your ass, Destiny. I'm not playing with you. Get the fuck on!" I yelled and looked up to see my brother pulling up to my house. From where I was standing, I could see him entering the code into the gate and making his way through the iron rails.

My new property was ducked off on the north side of Dallas in a gated community that was filled with prestigious houses mostly owned by doctors, lawyers, and niggas like me that got it out the mud and the courtroom.

"Mmgh, there's your bitch ass, punk ass brother. He tells you anything and you listen to him. Couldn't even keep his own damn wife, yet he has the nerve to butt his nose in our relationship. You let him do this to us, KaeDee."

"I didn't let him do shit. You did this to yourself when you were caught trying to send him to prison for that dope shit. You knew he wouldn't stop until your ass was gone," I said becoming more and more pissed off just thinking about how far this bitch was willing to go.

I slid my hands back into my pockets and sighed before I inhaled, then exhaled.

"Don't think I won't go further," Destiny threatened, as she stood to her feet and straightened out her clothes.

I snapped and quickly pulled my hands from my pockets and wrapped one around her throat while pointing a finger in her face. I gritted down on my bottom lip and sneered as I stared into her eyes. I guess she didn't know what I was capable of, being that I didn't see an ounce of fear behind her eyes. In a sense, that was my fault, because she had seen me at my weakest. Nights where I would cry out like a bitch for hours over losing Deonna, and she was right there to comfort me.

Those were times that I should've been on my toes and paying attention, because looking at her now, I saw how much I had been blind to. Her actions were misleading, and had I looked into her eyes, I would've seen how fucked up her soul was. My mama was always right about the eyes telling me and my brothers everything we needed to know on whether a woman was for us or not, and Deonna's eyes never led me to believe that she wasn't.

True, she had lied, cheated, and hid some things from me, but I was guilty of doing the same damn thing. I didn't tell her my true profession until we were married, and I had done my thing with a couple of women a time or two, so who was I to judge. I may have been mad, in my feelings, and acted off impulse for a little bit, but losing Deonna would've never been my choice. I would've forgiven and continued to love on the lady I chose to give my last name just like I had when I found out she had fucked Tyrin.

I knew in my heart that Deonna would never do anything to ever fuck over me again. I saw and felt the way she loved me after we had decided to reconcile and salvage our marriage. She treated me and our daughter like we were the most important things in her life. She was love for real, and Destiny had no right to take that away from me and the kid.

"Let her go! Let her go! Let her go!" Khi said, once he ran upon us and tried to pull my hand from around Destiny's neck. I only tightened the grip, angry that I had allowed this bitch in. She was someone that I never thought I would love, but I did, and that had been my biggest regret.

"Bruh, let her go! Cass done got locked up; he needs you," was all Khi had to say to bring me to my senses.

I let Destiny go and shoved her forward causing her to stumble and fall to the ground. Khi walked over to her and pulled her up from the ground, and the two of them stared at each other, I'm sure having the same thoughts about each other. Khi had been wanting to body Destiny, but I had always came to her defense, laughed it off, and told him to leave her alone. Now that I knew that she was the reason behind Khi's arrest a couple of months back, I knew it was going to be nothing that I could do to stop him from what he was going to do to her.

Khi didn't let shit get in the way of his bread, and he had proved to us all when he had sent our own little brother to jail for getting too out of pocket. I could only imagine what he would do once he found out about this shit. I halfway wanted to keep the shit to myself for the sake of the unborn child Destiny was carrying, but it was only a matter of time before he found out anyway. The nigga had smartened up and hired Destiny's partner, putting her on payroll to keep him five steps ahead of anything that had the Prince name in the mix.

"Let's go," I said to Khi, as I watched him bite down on his lip with half a smirk planted across his face, while he stared at Destiny.

"I'm a see you later, you know that right," Khi chuckled, as he stepped away from Destiny and placed his hands into his pockets. He had just confirmed that he knew, which meant that Agent Warren, Destiny's partner, was doing her muthafuckin' job. A little part of me felt bad, but I had hoped that I could convince this nigga to at least wait until my damn seed was born.

I turned away to walk inside of the house, quickly grabbed my keys, and headed right back out to hop in the car with Khi. As soon as he got in, he ran his hands over his face and looked at me.

"Don't even say it nigga. I already know," I told him, and he tossed the car in drive and sped off down the driveway.

"She played you nigga. Just like Deonna. You and these twisted ass women you like," Khi said, and I scoffed. "Tangie had the baby a few hours ago."

"Cass wasn't there?" I asked, and Khi shook his head. "Fuck did he got locked up for this time?"

"Murder. Went down there and police talking about they found Jourdin's body wrapped up in a blanket in an abandoned house. She had been beaten damn near beyond recognition."

"Jourdin? Everybody said she ran off," I said and sighed.

"Everybody like who...Cass? Cass told everybody she ran off. He takes care of Jourdin's grandma 'cause he knew Jourdin was never coming back. I just wish that nigga had told me what was up. We could've made sure this shit had never come back on him like this," Khi said, and I nodded.

"I'mma take care of it. I won't let him go back to prison, and that's my word fam. We've come too far. All of us are home, and we gotta do whatever we gotta do to keep it that way. We running this shit now, and everybody want us out the way, but we gotta make sure that nothing gets in the way of that."

"Like your baby mama," Khi said, and his glare shot in my direction before he looked back at the road.

"She's pregnant."

"Probably ain't even your kid."

"But it probably is."

"I had just dropped off some dope that day. I could've been locked up and gone. That wouldn't have been shit that you could've talked away KaeDee. That bitch is a liability, and she got too many muthafuckin' tricks up her sleeves. You better handle that hoe, KaeDee, 'cause you know I won't hesitate to body that hoe and drop her off in front of the FEDs doorstep."

"I was gonna tell you...I know you got your peoples informing you of shit, but I was gonna let you know that I knew what was up. I had just found out that everything you told me before, plus more, only a few hours ago. That muthafuckin' P.I. that works for my firm had been watching her for a couple of months now, and he laid her shit bare. Can't believe that bitch, man."

"Shit, why can't you? I told you that police ass hoe was flawed. You gonna start listening to your little brother, nigga," Khi said and chuckled. He pulled a blunt from his console and fired it up before cracking the window a bit.

"What my sis-in-law up to? Still giving you the blues?" I asked, and Khi frowned before hitting the weed.

"She still ain't trying to hear shit I got to say. Think she lied to me about what happened when Chaison had snatched her and Emon up."

"Why you say that?"

"Because when I went to pick her up to take her to the hospital with Tangie, I walked in on her changing clothes and saw a long ass scratch down her back that wasn't there before," Khi said and tried to offer me the weed, but I declined.

"You try talking to Emon again about it?" I asked him, and he shook his head.

"That nigga still mad at me. I told him I would help him get a new car and put him in his own spot, and next thing I knew, he was riding in a new Mazi and living with Cass. He ain't fuckin' with me...at all."

"He gonna come around. Just don't give up on him," I told Khi, and he nodded. I sat back in my seat and took my attention out of my window while Khi sped down the freeway. At this point in my life, I had always thought that my life would be written. Me and Deonna would have another baby by now, and we would still be running shit in the courtroom.

When that didn't happen, I somewhat assumed that me and Destiny were gonna run shit our way. Her ass didn't mind getting her hands dirty for me when I needed, and that alone had me thinking that she was worthy of marriage, but since I had found out who she really was, there I was all alone again. I needed and wanted somebody so bad. Somebody that was gonna ride for me for real. Somebody that would be forever and not with the shits.

Damn, a nigga just wanted a bad bitch who was a rider and who could be a good mother to the kid, I thought just as we pulled up to the police station and parked in an open spot.

"Let me go in here and find out what they know and get this nigga out of here. I will not...and I mean will not let him go down behind this shit," I promised, as I slapped hands with Khi and got out of the car.

I pulled off the shirt I was wearing and tossed it into the car only wearing a white t-shirt, a pair of Lacoste jeans, and my workout tennis that I had thrown on just to throw Destiny out of my house. I was dressed down and far from what I normally looked like whenever I had to come to the police station, but it didn't matter though. No matter what I looked like, I was still Attorney KaeDee Prince and brothers' freedom was golden to me.

Since failing them all in the past, I vowed to never allow it to happen again in the present or future, and my word was bond.

4

KHI

"Kind of tired; you mind if I come inside," I asked Cuba the moment I pulled into her driveway and placed the car in park. I leaned back in my seat and looked over at her; she wasn't the same woman that I had met almost two years ago. She had grown into her natural state of beauty even more, and had completely shed that hard ass shell that she called herself using to keep me and any other nigga out. I was persistent back then to have her just as I was now. Besides the kids and my brothers, Cuba was all I had. She was the only thing that could fill that void that I was missing in my life.

I hated that I had fucked up with her, but that shit with Selena was way back when me and Cuba wasn't even really serious. She was still running from a nigga, and I had a few minutes of weakness that led to not shit. I don't know who the fuck Selena's son's father was, but it wasn't me, and I couldn't get Cuba to look past that shit for nothing. She was dead set on making me pay for every fuckin' mistake that I had made, especially being that the last one led to her being snatched up by Chaison.

No matter how many times I apologized and stopped at nothing until I had brought my shawty and brother home, it was in one ear and out the other with Cuba. She wasn't hearing shit. I had pleaded for at least two months straight, buying gifts and pulling out every card to show her how sorry I was and how much I had appreciated her, but this time, none of it worked. Cuba was mad at me...so mad that she no longer cared that I had even used Sky against her to try to get her to come back to me. She had enough of my shit, but I wasn't the losing type and would do anything to win.

"Call Mario or somebody to come pick you up," Cuba said and rushed out of the car. I quickly dead the engine and hopped out behind her, following her up the steps that led to her front door. Once she unlocked the door and opened it, she tried to step inside and shut me out, but I stuck my foot out and stopped her.

"Khi, go away. I'm exhausted...just leave me alone, okay?" Cuba said, and I stepped inside of her home and closed and locked the door behind me.

"I ain't gonna bother you. I just wanna get some rest. I'll sleep in one of the guest bedrooms so you won't even know I'm here," I told her, and she rolled her eyes and turned around to walk away. I walked through Cuba's spot and made my way into one of the guest bedrooms that was closest to her bedroom. Sitting on the bed, I pulled out a cigar and a bag of weed and commenced to rolling up. As soon as I was done, I lit the tip and made my way to Cuba's room. She didn't lock the door like she had done many times before when I used the I was tired excuse to come and spend the night with her.

"Ughhh," Cuba grunted, when I pushed the door open and stepped inside of her room. "I forgot to lock it this time."

"You knew it wouldn't have stopped me any damn way," I told her, as I blew out a cloud of smoke and walked over to her bed to sit down. "Tangie good?"

"Yea."

"You good?"

"Yep."

"Mean ass. You know I ain't gonna stop, right?"

"I wish that you would, Khi. Damn."

"I slept with that bitch one fuckin' time! How many times I gotta say I'm sorry for some shit that didn't mean a muthafuckin' thing to me? And then you see the hoe was lying about that damn baby being mine."

"It's not about if it meant anything to you or not; it's about if I ever meant anything to you. You married me because you knew that, when I found out, I would never leave you."

"No the fuck I didn't! I married you cause I wanted to be with you. Man, come on! Everybody know how I feel about you, Cuba. Why the fuck you the only one that can't see it?"

"My God, can you just leave me alone, Khi. I don't wanna talk about this right now."

"What you want me to do that I haven't done already? Please just tell me," I pleaded. I walked around to Cuba's side of the bed and kneeled down in front of where she sat. I toked in a good amount of the hay before I placed the tip of the blunt to my lips and looked up at Cuba. I saw the tears that were forming in the corner of her eyes, and I knew that meant she still cared for a nigga no matter how hard she tried not to. Anytime I was around her she was crying, and all I wanted to do was turn those tears into ones of joy instead of pain. I was a nigga and the type that would admit when I was wrong and try to fix that shit if the person I hurt meant anything to me. Cuba meant the world to me, and I would give her the world just to see her smile again.

"You haven't left me alone yet. That's what I want you to do," Cuba answered, and I sighed and sat the blunt on her nightstand.

"You sure about that? You want me to let you go...give you that divorce you keep asking for."

"Yep, definitely."

"You know that means, when I walk away, I ain't ever coming back, right?"

"I'm fine with that," Cuba said, and I stood to my feet.

"A'ight, and soon as I get married again and get another chick pregnant since your hoe ass couldn't be woman enough to have my damn seed, then don't come to me crying."

"Any bitch that has a baby by your coward ass is a damn fool. You don't protect your woman or your kids, so it won't be shit for me to cry about."

I swallowed back and slid my hands deep into the pockets of my sweats. I looked down at Cuba, tears spilling from her eyes, and her lip quivering. I nodded before I grabbed my blunt and walked out of her room and headed to my car. As soon as I sat down in the driver's seat, I slammed my fist into the steering wheel and just sat there for a moment thinking about what Cuba had just said to me. I needed to get Emon to talk to me. Something had happened when Chaison had Cuba and him locked up, and I had to get Emon to tell me exactly what since I knew Cuba never would.

~

"Hey, bruh! Let me holla at you for a minute," I called out to Emon, who was all cheesing in a baddie's face until he saw me approaching him. Quickly, his smile turned into a frown, and he grabbed his keys and walked around to the driver's side of his Mazi. I jogged a little to catch up to him and hurried to grab him before he could get inside of the car. "Hold up, nigga, you don't hear me talking to you."

"What the fuck you want?" Emon sighed, and I gritted as I stared at him. He had been mad at me ever since Chaison snatched his ass up too. Mainly because he'd found out that I had known all along about his relationship to Chaison, and that he wasn't our pops' biological child. I could understand that nigga being in his feelings, but I did what I had to do to protect him. Plus, that shit didn't matter to me. Emon was my little brother no matter what, and although we didn't share the same father, we came from the same womb. Nothing would ever change how I felt about him. He was still my little nigga that I had practically had a hand in raising, which was why I wasn't about to keep letting this nigga keep disrespecting me.

Three months was long enough to hold a grudge, but now it was time for this nigga to man the fuck up and get over that shit.

I slapped Emon across the face and then walked up closer to him, my chest to his and me daring that nigga to do something about it.

Emon was about 5'11 and a good hundred and seventy-five pounds. He didn't look too much like the rest of us except his skin tone. He was dark-skinned with the same build, but he didn't have the signature hazel eyes or the lips we had gotten from our pops. Emon wore his hair in a box type style with some fucked up looking twist-like shit on top of his head that all these new generations of youngins was rocking. I hated that shit, but he kept a fresh line-up and kept it neat so it wasn't as bad as a lot of the kids I had been seeing.

"Fuck is wrong with you, Khian," Emon said, and I sucked my teeth and grabbed him by the collar of his shirt. I looked into his eyes seeing that I had really pissed him off. His chest heaved up and down, and his spit was gathering on the sides of his mouth.

"You must think because you did that little bid that you can whoop me or something? You keep talking to me like I'm some hoe ass nigga in these streets tho, we gonna see what them hands looking like."

"Let me go, Khian," Emon spat, and I loosened the grip that I had around him, then straightened his clothes out.

"Get in the car; I need to talk to you," I told him, and he mugged me before looking around me at the little chick he had been talking to. "That's your, shawty?"

"Yasline, I'll holla at you later," Emon told her and opened the door to his car and got inside. I walked around to the passenger's side and fell into the peanut butter leather seats.

"Yasline. She's a baddie," I said, as I watched Emon's little girlfriend walk away.

"What's up?"

"Look, little nigga. I apologize for not telling you about your peoples, but no lie, I was gonna take that shit to my grave just like pops and mama was. It didn't matter to them, and that shit don't matter to me or any of us. Nigga you still a Prince, so why you even letting that shit get to you, bruh? Pops never treated you no differently and been knowing since you was born that you wasn't yours biologically. That nigga didn't care. I don't care. KaeDee, Cass, or Dae don't give a damn. You still ours. The fuck is you mad for?" I yelled and looked over at Emon and could see him loosening up just a little. He sighed and leaned back in his seat while keeping his stare out the front window.

"I'm scraight," he said and glanced over at me. "I traded up the minute I put a bullet in Amrin and that nigga Turner. Had you not popped Chaison, I would've bodied that nigga, too. That's my mutha-fuckin' family, and trust me, I ain't mad."

"Oh, you ain't mad? So you've been avoiding me because of what then?"

"I ain't been avoiding you, nigga. I'm adjusting and just chillin," Emon said, and I nodded.

"What's up, then? Talk to me," I told Emon, and he looked at me and frowned.

"Talk to you about what?" he asked with a confused look on his face.

"Chaison...what happened with you and Cuba?"

"Lady at the jailhouse called an Uber, Chaison showed up, and my dumb ass got inside thinking he was my ride. He snatched Cuba up off the side of the road, and y'all came through that bitch days later on some ninja type shit and saved the muthafuckin' day. Ain't shit to talk about. It is what it is."

"How did Cuba get that scar on her back? She told me nothing happened to her, but I know that it wasn't there before all this shit happened. Now, I know why she wouldn't let me come inside her hospital room, touch her afterwards, never let me see her naked...shit nothing."

"Oh...I don't know nothing about no scar," Emon said lightly. I looked over at him as he stared out of his window seeming to be in deep thought.

"Did that nigga Chaison do that shit to her?" I asked and Emon shrugged. "You don't know or just don't wanna say?"

"I wasn't in the same room with her, so I don't know what happened."

"But you was in the same room when we found y'all."

"Just for that day," Emon said, and I knew he was lying.

"Just want my wife back and the same bond I had with my little brother before he got locked up."

"I promised her I wouldn't tell," Emon said and sighed.

"Who is your loyalty with? Me or her?" I asked, and Emon looked at me.

"My loyalty...is with you."

5

CASSIDY

"Aww, what's the matter C.J.," Tangie said, as I peeked in on her and the kid. I shook my head and ran my hands across my face watching her interact with my first and only biological child— well my first living child. This was the second time I had missed the birth of one of my shawties, and that shit was eating me up inside, but I had gotten caught up, and Tangie wasn't even supposed to be due yet. I never anticipated being stuck with murder charges behind that bitch Jourdin, but thank God for the bruh for coming through like he had. I wasn't in the clear on them charges yet, but KaeDee had bought me a little time to fix this shit up so it was nothing for me to worry about in the future.

As far as Jourdin and what happened to her...yea, I was the one that put her in that little situation. She'd tried to play me, and I made sure I got her right for it. Shit was fucked up what she had done. From the beginning, I had denied that Cassie was even mine. I was dead-set on that shit, because I knew what type of lifestyle Jourdin lived, but when I came home and laid my eyes on that little girl, it was no denying the evident.

Jourdin's ol' slick ass had really thought that shit through. She knew my condition with my eyes was very rare, and that I would never question her. I had fell in love at first sight the moment I laid my eyes on Cassie. That little girl had become my heart, and I would do whatever I had to do to protect the kid. Regardless of what her hoe ass mama did, she was a Prince and she would always be one.

Tangie had stepped up in her mama's place after I told her that Jourdin told me to take Cassie with me that night and that she was leaving to be with some nigga. Of course, Tangie thought that it was only going to be temporary, because she couldn't see how a mother could ever leave her child, but with each day, she saw that shit was real. Jourdin was never coming back, and the only thing I could do now was convince Tangie that I had nothing to do with Jourdin's death and ensure that she never found out that Cassie wasn't really mine.

"Hey..." I said catching Tangie's attention. She had gotten up from her hospital bed ready to lay our son down when I stepped inside of the room and held my hands out for him. Tangie, for a minute, looked upset, but she gently laid him into my arms and walked away to the bathroom.

I found a chair in the corner of the room and sat down so that I could look the kid over. Not gonna lie, ever since I found out about Cassie and the shit Jourdin had done, I had been on edge wondering if this little nigga that Tangie carried was mine. I knew that Tangie wasn't even like that—would never sleep around on a nigga, but it was always the what-ifs that fucked with me. What if she had found a nigga to lick her wounds when I was out there fucking up and he slipped up and got her pregnant just for her to put the shit back on me? Bitches could be slick and I ain't have a lot of trust for nobody right now.

"Yea, they're two different colors. The nurse said they might change, but I told her how you were, and they been in here snapping pictures ever since."

"Can't believe the little nigga got his eyes open already," I chuckled. "He alert as fuck right now. And hungry."

"I just fed him like twenty minutes ago. That's all I've been doing since he came out. I'm tempted to give up on breastfeeding and give him a bottle since I haven't slept since I had him," Tangie said, her voice sounding strained and groggy.

"I got him baby; get you some rest," I told her and grabbed her hand. I stood to my feet and leaned over and kissed her little short ass on the forehead. "I'm sorry, a'ight. Everything gonna be cool, though."

"Is it Cass? You out here killing people as if I'm not already one child that has lost a mother that apparently you killed," Tangie said and I frowned.

"Fuck is you talking about? I didn't kill no damn body, and if I did, you really think I would do that shit to Jourdin?"

"Cass...please don't. You and both know that it doesn't matter if you did or didn't do it. All that matters is that they said you did. What the fuck am I supposed to do if you got locked up again, Cass? You out here making decisions that's gonna have me a single fuckin' parent, and I wish you would ask me to wait for you. Just think about how I brought one child into this world that was already dead without you, and now the son that we prayed for; I had to do that shit alone as well."

"You acting like I got arrested on purpose or something, and damn, you wasn't even due until next month. You know damn well I would've been here for the kid. Don't even play me like that. Soon as you sent the text and said your water broke, I was on my way and got rolled by twelve."

"Where were you, anyway?"

"Chmmp, man don't even start," I said and sighed. I sat back down and looked into my son's face. He was white as fuck and had a head full of straight black hair. I felt better knowing the kid had the funny looking eyes, and it hadn't even been twenty-four hours yet that he'd been here. One thing I knew for certain was that these wasn't no contacts. He was mine for sure, and I was gonna raise him to reach his fullest potential. I was fucked up, some shit due to my environment, but he didn't have to go through none of what I did.

The little nigga is gonna be a king…a Prince, I thought, as I smiled while rubbing my hand over his little head.

"How much did he weigh? Dude is kinda big to be early?" I asked and looked up at Tangie. Tears stained her face, and I sighed and stood up so that I can sit on the hospital bed with her.

"He was seven-and-a-half-pounds and twenty-two inches long. Too big for me to push out," Tangie said, and I looked down at her before sitting next to her.

"What you mean?"

"I had to get a C-Section, Cass. They cut me open, and had it not been for Cuba and Emon being there for me, I would've had to endure that alone. Shit, I still felt alone, and that was a terrible feeling. Cass, please don't leave me. Please tell me you're not about to go to jail again?" Tangie pleaded, and I wrapped my arm around her and pulled her into my chest. I kissed her on her forehead just as my phone vibrated in my pocket. When I pulled out, I saw a series of text messages from Khi on my lock screen.

Khi: Where you at?

Khi: We got an issue.

Khi: Problem at the bakery

"Fuck," I cursed under my breath and slid the phone back into my pocket. I kissed Tangie on her forehead again and chilled for a moment with her and the kid. I knew that Khi needed me, but that shit was gonna have to wait. Right now, I had a lot of making up to do after missing the birth of my son and having Tangie go through it all alone for the second damn time. Wasn't no way I was about to walk away from her right now.

"You good?" I asked her, and she nodded and snuggled up close to my chest.

"Yes, just tired," she said barely above a whisper.

"Go to sleep. I got him. I ain't going nowhere," I told her, and it wasn't long before she was dropping slob all down my damn shirt. After a few minutes of spoiling the youngin', I laid him in his little crib and walked over to the window. This little family thing with Tangie was something that I had always wanted. Even when I was locked up, I had dreamed over and over again of coming home to Tangie, fixing shit, and having a bunch of damn kids. I couldn't mess this up. It was already starting to feel like life was complete, except there was only one thing left to do.

6

DAELAN

Ding Dong! Ding Dong! Ding Dong!

"Why we gotta come home so early? You just came home, Daddy," D.J. whined, and I ran my hand across his head before pulling him into a headlock.

"My bad, little man. Something done came up, and daddy gotta go see about it, but I promise you, I'mma come pick you and your brother up and take y'all to see the next Mavericks game," I told him, and that got a smile out of him. I went to ring the doorbell again, when the door swung open, and some nigga stepped out of the house. I gritted down on my teeth and quickly stepped back to check shit out.

"Fuck is this?" I asked, looking from him to Amber. He was some light-skinned, square ass nigga that had on a pair of khaki slacks and a plaid-collared shirt. Nigga was a straight up lame, and seeing this nigga coming out the house where the kid rested his head was pissing me the fuck off. I tried like a muthafucka to get back with Amber.

Shit, had even thought we were back together until she told me she was ready to move out from KaeDee's place and into her own spot for just her and D.J.

We had been sleeping together, going out on little dates, I had accompanied her to a few of therapy sessions, and even took time out to take her to the park to train her myself so that she could get back to walking again. I swear it seemed like, as soon as she was able to move around like normal again, she was ready to get rid of me, and I ain't like that shit. I felt like she had used me, but I didn't even know if I had a right to be mad.

We never established if we were back together or not, but I guess a nigga had assumed that, when I would ask her whose pussy that was, and she would say mine, we were fucking dating again. I guess I had assumed wrong.

"Oh, hey Ronnie," D.J. said, and I sucked my teeth and pulled my dreads out of my face.

"Ronnie...fuck is Ronnie doing come out of here, and for how long have you known Ronnie, D.J.," I asked, and Amber pulled our son into the house, then looked at me and frowned.

"Don't question him, Dae. Go inside and put your things up, D.J. I'll be inside in a minute once I'm done seeing Ronnie out and saying goodbye to your father."

"Yea, see this nigga Ronnie out cause we gotta talk ASAP," I said, while keeping my stare on this cat.

"How you doing? I'm Ronnie," he held out his hand for me to shake as soon as DJ had gone inside, and I slid my hands into my pockets and frowned at that nigga. Fuck I look like.

"Don't mind him, babe. I'll see you later," Amber said and kissed him on the cheek and then his lips before the nigga walked off and headed to his car, which was a Honda; I hadn't even noticed it at first.

"Don't mind him, babe? Then, you kissing this nigga all in front of me. You got niggas around my son, Amber?"

"Niggas? No. I haven't had any niggas around your son, and the only reason you or DJ saw him here tonight is because you weren't supposed to be bringing him back until tomorrow."

"How does DJ know that dude if you haven't had him around?" I asked and crossed my arms over my chest.

"Because he's the soccer coach at DJ's school."

"Yea, like I thought, a straight up lame. At least you could've hooked up with the football coach. This nigga got his shirt all tucked in tight and shit. How the fuck I know this lame ass nigga not a fuckin' child molester. Tight ass khaki pants and shit, really, Amber?"

"You're overreacting, Daelan. Just because he isn't some damn dope boy walking around with his pants to his knees don't mean he's a lame. Besides, you should be happy that I have a decent male-figure around."

"Happy...the fuck? I just fucked you last week, Amber!"

"So, what. Keep your damn voice down before DJ hears you."

"Fucked up part about it is, I don't even know if I'm being cheated on or not. Am I the side nigga?" I asked, and Amber laughed like something was funny, but I was dead ass serious. I now knew how chicks felt when they found out their nigga was sleeping around with another bitch. This shit had me fucked up in the head, for real.

"You are so damn silly. You and I are not together, and Ronnie and I aren't either. I'm dating...doing me...you know, how you did for the duration of our relationship. I'm learning about who Amber is and what Amber likes, and I'm happy. Don't come over here no more acting rude in front of my company. This was exactly why I said I will pay my own damn bills, because I knew your ass was gonna get to tripping. Bye, Daelan."

"Damn...this fucked up," I said and backed away. I ain't even know what to say. Amber was lucky that I was a changed man, and that I was trying and doing everything to stay that way. I could've slapped fye from her ass for doing some shit like this, but I had promised her, DJ, and myself that I would never lay hands on her again. A nigga really wanted his family back together, but if Amber wasn't trying to hear that shit, then fuck it, I would just move on.

"Sorry, Daelan, but too much has transpired, and I just...I just can't look at you without thinking about everything that happened to me. Just know that I'll always love you."

"It's cool, Ma. Do your thang. Just be careful who you have around the kid, ya hear? Me and you both know that you can't trust niggas," I told her and turned around to head to my car. I pulled down open, fell inside, and quickly cranked the engine. Future's "Codeine Crazy" started blasting from the speakers, and I sped out of the driveway and onto the dark streets.

Pour that bubbly, drink that muddy drink that muddy drink, that muddy. When we're cuddling, yea I'm covered in. I was thuggin it, I was just loving it. That's for them other niggas.

I bobbed my head as I cruised down the streets headed to meet up with Khi and Cassidy about some shit that popped off just after I had gotten home. I really couldn't even be mad at Amber though honestly. I was out here deep at this shit damn near 24/7 trying to make up for everything that I had fucked up, and to show my brothers that I was about this dope shit.

I only really got to spend a good day out of the week with the kid, sometimes two if someone else made drop-offs. Even then, that time had to be combined with the time I had to spend with BJ, and my newborn son, Dylan, that I had with Taylana. I didn't even fuckin' have time to be a family man, and I knew that was what Amber wanted. She wanted a nigga to be out of the streets and to square up, and right now, that just wasn't my life. I had too much to do and accomplish before I could just get out the game and move out the way for the next nigga to come along and take over. There was money to be made, so I might as well get it just so my kids could be rich forever.

I wasn't even gonna trip with Amber; I was going to let her do her thang. Shit, she deserved a nigga to make her happy. I had fucked up her heart and her head, and she was walking around with a permanent limp because of my shit. I was somewhat salty that I couldn't be the one to fix it all, but I would gracefully bow out of this one.

Taylana and I were on good terms, doing our little co-parenting thing and making sure we kept shit friendly. I thought I was gonna have to fuck that girl up, but after enough times of me going to her brother, she had finally left a nigga alone. Hopefully, she would have a boyfriend soon, shit. I would even help her find one if she needed me to.

After a good thirty minutes of driving, I pulled into an abandoned car lot and drove around to the back of the building. I spotted Khi, Emon, and KaeDee parked against the brick wall and slowly made my way over to the them. Placing the car in park, I dead the engine, got out, and walked over to my brothers.

"What up, fam," I said to KaeDee, as I dapped him up and gave him a hug. I did the same for Khi and Emon, and then leaned back on the hood of Khi's new Bentley.

"Cass ain't gonna make it out here, but we gotta little situation. That nigga Tamar hit me up talking about the package that Dae dropped off last night was intercepted by the FEDs right after you turned it over. They got all that shit and done arrested the niggas that took over."

"Oh, fuck, is you serious?" I asked and pulled my dreads from my face. I hiked my pants up a couple of inches and then started to pace back and forth. "Who is these niggas though? Is they gonna snitch on the kid or what, bruh?"

"I don't know. KaeDee bout to go look into it, and then I got that lil' police bitch Aisha doing her thang too, but don't even worry, my nigga, because this gonna be all on me. I told KaeDee and Aisha to make sure of that."

"What?" both me and Emon said at the same time.

"Hell, nah; we in this together," I said and walked over to my car, then pulled the door open. Damn, a nigga couldn't even shine for too long before the hate started coming. We hadn't even been the front runners but for a hot minute, and we already got the FEDs trying to bring us down. I was for sure it was because of some hating ass bitch or nigga, too. We wasn't even making that much noise for the FEDs to be in our backyards like that.

"That's how I feel. We all benefitting from this shit, so if one goes down, then we all go down," Emon said just as I walked back over to them with a blunt hanging from the tip of my mouth and my dreads hanging down my face. I took in a good amount of the hay and then looked up at KaeDee.

"You down for this shit? You told him yes?" I asked KaeDee, and he looked at me and frowned.

"Nah, I ain't down for shit, little nigga. I told Khi that I was gonna fix this, but you know how he is."

"I'm saying though, Emon, you just got out, and after what happened with you the last time Dae, nah bruh. I got this. If anybody goes down, it's gonna be me," Khi said, and I shook my head profusely.

Nah, I wasn't having that. This nigga had taken care of all of us since we had been little youngins, and even though we butted heads often, I had nothing but love for the bruh. I would take a bullet over and over again for Khi. A nigga wasn't even tripping no more about him getting me locked up, because it had changed me for the better, and I knew that was the only reason he had done it. I knew for sure I would probably be dead or even serving a life sentence if he hadn't made the move he'd made. Khi was thorough, and with him, it was family above all else. It always had been. Without Khi, we all would fall the fuck apart. It wouldn't be Prince brothers nothing.

"What about your wife? The kid?"

"Cuba will be good, and I know she'll take care Sky so that's nothing."

"Man, we not even gonna claim this shit. Y'all niggas is talking like y'all know they gonna snitch. How about we just find out who these niggas is and hit they ass with this fye," Emon said, and I nodded, agreeing with everything he had said.

"Yea...yea, let's do that. Like, ASAP. I'm wit it," I said and passed the blunt over to Emon. I nodded my head and started rubbing my hands together like Birdman.

"Y'all niggas just itching to slump somebody. I knew it wasn't gonna be nothing nice when y'all asses got back together," Khi said, and KaeDee chuckled and shook his head. "Let's get to it then. I should have some names by morning."

I nodded and so did Emon. We stood behind the building chopping it up for a few minutes while passing the hay around before we all went our separate ways. It was go time.

7

CUBA

"Please! Please no! Get off of me!" I screamed at the top of my lungs and did my best to fight Chaison off of me. I kicked and punched, and when that wasn't enough, I dug my teeth into his arm and bit down as hard as I could. For a minute, that got him and caused his arms to go weak, so I used that as my opportunity to get away from him. I slid underneath him, hopped up, and ran towards where Emon was helplessly tied in the corner of the room.

"Come on; we gotta go!" I screamed, noticing that Emon's eyes went over my shoulder. I turned around to see what he was looking at just in time to see Chaison.

"You bitch!" he yelled and brought his hand up over his head.

"Nooooooo!"

Ding Dong! Ding Dong! Ding Dong!

I jumped up at the sound of my doorbell ringing and hurried and got out of bed to answer it. Once I opened the door, I tossed my hand on my side and sucked my teeth. I should've known that it wasn't nobody but Khi's ass being that he was the only fool that showed up in the middle of the night not giving a damn if he was invited or not. I rolled my eyes at him and reached out for Skylarr who was sleeping peacefully on his chest.

"Thought you wasn't gonna let me see her anymore," I said to him, and he handed her to me before walking inside of my home and over to my sofa. I closed my door and locked it, and then, took Skylarr to the bedroom that I had set up for her and my nephew BJ. After tucking her in the bed, I turned on the nightlight and cracked the door before going back to where Khi had gotten entirely too comfortable.

"I should've never done that. Take her away from you like that. She's been asking for you like crazy, and I was in my feelings. I apologize," Khi said while looking up at me. I nodded my head but didn't know what to say. I just hoped that he wasn't gonna turn around and take her away from me whenever he got mad again.

"Thank you. So does this mean that she can live with me?" I asked him, and he nodded his head and sighed. I could see that something was really, really bothering him, and although I wanted to be a mean bitch to him as usual, I couldn't. I walked over to the loveseat across from him and sat down. "Are you okay?"

"Just take care of her. I don't trust her with nobody but you. If I get locked up...just make sure you bring her to see me from time to time. Don't let her forget who I am."

"What? What you mean?"

"Found out today that some niggas out in Memphis got knocked and snitched on me," Khi said and chuckled. "I ain't never met these niggas a day in my damn life. This the first time we even did business with these cats. Dae went down there to drop off a shipment, and soon as they take off with that shit, they was knocked by the FEDs. They gave up me and another nigga from the Chi. Twenty-six bricks of un-stepped on coke."

"Oh, my God. Khi...I'm sorry. I mean...what...what. Shit, I don't know what to say. I'm sorry. Is there anything you can do? How did they get your name? I don't understand. Why would they tell on you and not Dae?"

"I don't even fuckin' know. But I would rather them give up my name than my little brother. Dae ain't built to be behind them walls man," Khi said, and I looked at him like he was crazy.

"I swear, you always putting them niggas over you. What about your family?" I said, suddenly becoming emotional.

"What family? You mean this shit here? My fuckin' wife that keeps running away from me...killed my muthafuckin' seed. You mean that family?" Khi asked causing tears to spill from my eyes. "Got no muthafuckin' family. Besides, I know you'll take good fuckin' care of my daughter and Selena will take good care of Kenya."

"I'm sorry, Khi. You don't have to keep throwing that shit in my damn face. I know I killed your child, and I swear, I regret it every day, but I was just going through so much."

"Yea, I know. You always go through something let you tell it. You make mistakes like a muthafucka, but I ain't never ran away from you and made you pay for that shit. I still was right here trying to do whatever I had to do to make this shit work with you. A nigga make one fuckin mistake, and you screaming for a damn divorce! Had I known I didn't have a rider on my damn hands, I would've never married your ass."

"Really, Khi? A rider? What the fuck have you suffered from? Every mistake you made, I suffered because of it. Your baby mama tried to turn me into a fuckin' dopefiend, then Selena! Because of that shit, it led to me getting raped and beat by one of your fuckin' enemies!" I screamed and stood up from the couch. I took off running towards my bedroom and into the bathroom.

Shit; I thought to myself not believing I had just said that shit. I had vowed to never tell a soul what happened, not even Tangie. I had even begged Emon not to say anything. I was so embarrassed by what happened... felt so disgusted, especially being that it happened right in front of Emon. He promised that he would never tell anyone, and as far as I knew, he had kept his word. I knew that Khi had been fishing for info, because Emon had text me to tell me that he'd made up some false story about Chaison slapping me around a few times. He said that Chaison had hit me so hard one time that it caused me to stumble backwards and hit my back on the way causing the scar that I had. It wasn't the truth, but I wished like hell that it was.

"Open the door! Open the fuckin' door before I kick it down,

Cuba!" Khi yelled, and I rushed over to the toilet, pulled up the lid, and vomited. I coughed uncontrollably before more of my stomach's contents spilled out into the toilet. Behind me, I could hear Khi pushing on the door over and over again. I sucked in a deep breath and held my mouth closed hoping that nothing else would come up. When I stood to my feet, Khi had pushed the door open with force popping the lock and breaking the little latch that had secured everything shut.

"I...I..." I tried to say something, but nothing would come out but cries followed by a painful scream. Khi rushed to me and pulled me into his arms. This time, I didn't fight him and allowed him to comfort me. Every night, I went to bed lonely, followed by nightmares of everything that went down when Chaison kidnapped me and Emon. It was probably the most horrific thing that had ever happened to me, and even though I placed blame on Khi for it, it wasn't his fault.

He'd told me time and time again not to ever leave the house without him or one of his goonies accompanying me, and I had allowed my emotions to cause me to think irrationally. He knew that there was danger lurking out there, and that someone was waiting to use me to get to him, and he wasn't wrong. As soon as I got a good few miles away from the house, there was Chaison. I had given him the perfect opportunity to make Khi pay for whatever he had done to him.

"I'm so sorry. Damn, I'm sorry," Khi said to me, his voice cracking as he spoke. He held onto me tightly while allowing me to cry into his chest. I never wanted him to know that this happened to me, which was why I wouldn't even allow him to come into my hospital room when they had found me. I had even told the hospital staff that he was not allowed to have access to my records, because we were getting a divorce. Khi didn't see me until after I was released, and the moment we came home, I ran off and let Khi know that I no longer wanted to be with him.

At the time, he was the blame. The situation with Selena was still fresh in my mind, and shit, had it not been for that, then there would've been no reason for me to run off. Even then, I still had to accept my part in this. Khi was right though. Anytime there was some type of issue with us, I ran. Me running was what led him to sleeping with Selena in the first place. Not saying that it was right for him to do it, but damn if I hadn't, would he had still slept with her?

"I never wanted you to know," I said, and Khi pulled me away from me and forced me to look up at him. He took the back of his hand and wiped away the tears that stained my face before wiping away the ones that had spilled onto his cheek. Seeing him crying for me hurt me to my core. Damn, he really does love me; I thought to myself and tried to hold my head down, but Khi leaned over and kissed my lips. I wanted to turn away from him, run as usual, but he held my head into place and forced his tongue into my mouth. I relaxed and allowed his tongue to dance with mine.

Khi picked me up from the floor and carried me into my bedroom. He sat me on the bed and knelt down in front of me while looking up at me. For a few moments, nothing was said between either of us. I didn't know what to say, or rather, I didn't know how to say what I felt. I just knew that, deep down, I still loved Khi, but it was just soooo much shit between us. No, he was not at fault for what others did, but he was still at fault for his actions that led them to do it in the first place.

Khi needed to know that, if he wanted me to stop running, he needed to make me feel secure enough to know that no matter what he had my back. He was always putting other people before me and that shit was unacceptable.

"I promise you that shit with Selena happened that one time, and I left her ass at that damn hotel after it happened. She went back to where her mama was, and I didn't hear from her until her ass was damn near halfway done with that pregnancy. She wanted to tell you, and I kept telling her no because I didn't believe it was mine. That shit with her was nothing to me. I promise you, all those times I went to see my child, I never fucked her. Not once."

"I don't understand why you couldn't just tell me that. You made me look stupid. And you was rushing to marry me...I felt like it was all because you were trying to lock me down for when I did find out."

"Come on now, I know won't shit lock you down married or not. Shit look where we at now. You still left didn't you," Khi said, and I wiped my face again and sighed. "I rushed to marry you cause I didn't want you leaving me again. I felt like if you knew that I was serious about wanting to be wit you then you would stop running from a nigga. I was eager to lock you down for that reason only...and I wanted you pregnant again."

I shook my head and looked over at the digital clock that sat on my nightstand. It was damn near five in the morning, and I had to be to work in three hours. Even though Khi paid for this house with his own money, I still liked working so that I could generate my own income. I had opened up an interior decorating firm and had successfully done work for about fifteen clients so far.

It was a slow process building up my client list, but things were coming along great, and I was happy doing what I did. Thankfully, Khi paid the bills on the office space as well, because I hadn't generated enough income to take care of it myself. He really looked out for me when it came to that. Khi wanted me to be successful and be my own woman, and I appreciated him for that.

"I gotta get up and go to the office tomorrow. I'm gonna take Sky with me until I can figure out what else to do with her on a day-to-day basis," I told Khi, and when I looked down at him, I could see him biting down on his bottom lip, which only meant he was thinking something freaky.

"You can't get your assistant to take over for today. I wanted to spend the day with you and Sky," Khi told me and kissed me on my thighs. I jumped at his touch and tried to back away from him.

"No...Khi, I need to go in myself. You know I'm trying to really get my shit popping," I told him, and he pulled me towards the edge of the bed and buried his between my legs.

"Baby, I'm sorry for everything. You all I got, Cuba. You and Sky the only people in this world that I give a fuck about at the end of the day. Tell me what I gotta do to have my family back together," Khi pleaded, and I sighed.

"You really hurt me, Khi."

"That ain't mean shit to me. I promise you it didn't. Here..." Khi went inside of the sweats that he was wearing and pulled out his cell phone. He entered the lock code and placed it in my lap. Looking up at me, I could see the desperation in his eyes. This was something that he really wanted, but I was confused about what I wanted. One day, I wanted him, and the next day, I hated him. One day, I was dead set on my decision to stay away from this nigga and to show him that Cuba was not to be walked over, but the next, I just wanted to lay on his chest while reading a book like old times.

"What am I supposed to do with this?" I asked him as I raised my brow.

"I ain't been talking to nobody. My shit dry as fuck. You see I still wear my fuckin' ring, and I don't say shit to Selena unless it's concerning Kenya," Khi told me, and I glanced at his phone before I pushed it away.

"I'm not about to be checking your phone. That's not even us."

"What I gotta do to prove to you that Selena didn't mean shit to me?"

"It's not about that, Khi. It's just the fact that you did it. How do I know that you won't do it again? What about the next bitch? Every time we have a problem, you gonna go and fuck some chick because we going through something."

"No...nah man, I ain't gonna do no shit like that. I love you too much for that. You got me scared as fuck man, and I swear I'll never do shit else to jeopardize what we got. You all I need baby, I just need you to stop running from me."

I sighed and looked into Khi's eyes. I believed him, but I was still scared. It was just something that I was just gonna have to work on. After the shit I went through with Rue and then all the drama with Khi, I couldn't just completely let my guard down. I had to protect myself some kind of way. I was gonna give Khi another chance, but for now, I was staying in my place. He wasn't gonna get me to just give my shit up that easily.

"Okay..." I said, causing Khi to further bite down on his bottom lip. He stood up to his feet and pulled the shirt over his head. I looked up at him and shook my head. Sex...last person that touched me in that way was Chaison. I wasn't sure if I was ready for this with Khi or not. "I don't know if...you know after..."

"Oh...yea...we ain't gotta do shit," Khi said. He pulled his sweats off and climbed in the bed with me, and then pulled me back with my chest into his back. "You good?"

"Yes, I'm okay," I said and closed my eyes. Khi gently kissed the back of my neck, and I let out a soft moan. He rubbed his hand up and down my thigh before sliding his tongue into my ear.

"I love you, Cuba. Never forget that," Khi told me, and I nodded my head.

"I love you too, Khi," I said to him and laid there while he kissed every part of my body while apologizing every few minutes until I drifted off to sleep.

8

KHI

Cuba laid in my arms lightly snoring while I laid there staring towards the ceiling. My insides burned with so much hate and anger. I had already put a bullet in that nigga Chaison, but knowing what I know now, I wish I could go back and do shit a totally different way. I knew something had to have happened to Cuba, but not once did I ever think it was some shit like this. I had accepted what Emon told me the other day, but now that I knew the truth, I wonder why he felt the need to lie to me. It had me thinking that there was still something that I didn't know, and at this point, I knew that I probably would never find out one hundred percent of everything.

Fuck; I thought to myself. Every time I thought about it, I heard the way Cuba screamed out in my head earlier. That shit was eating me up inside, and I knew it wasn't shit I could do to take that pain away from her. No matter what she said, though, I knew she blamed me for this shit. Hell, I blamed myself for it. I should've let Mario go after her that day when he asked me. I should've tried harder to take Chaison out, but damn, I didn't know he was gonna come at me like this.

"Mmmh," Cuba moaned in her sleep. I turned back over to my side and pulled her close to me again. I kissed her on her ear and then took my hand and gently raised her gown. The scar that was there was big and wide. Now that I was looking at it in more detail than I had before, I knew that it was something else that Emon was lying about. I knew there was no way she could've gotten this just by hitting the wall. It looked like there had been stitches there at one point and a lot of them.

Seeing my baby so frail like this made me wanna never leave her fuckin' side again. I wanted to hold onto her with one hand and keep a hammer in the other just to show her that I was gonna do my all to keep her unharmed. It was fucked up though that I might be going away. Shit was crazy as fuck. I hadn't even told the full truth to Dae, Emon, Cassidy about the fact that I had already been named as the Connect. Muthafuckas had quickly pointed me out, and KaeDee said that it was only a matter of time before the FEDs was beating down my door.

I knew it was some more shit with this, because I had never even met them niggas, and as far as I knew, they didn't even know Dae. The way the shit was supposed to work was Dae was supposed to drop the load off at an agreed upon location, leave the keys in the truck, and leave the scene. He would be ducked off and waiting for the niggas to pick up the truck and take pictures of them getting inside in case they wanted to come back and say that they never got their load.

Nine times out of ten, they were just workers like what we were supposed to have, and them niggas wasn't supposed to know shit about us, but somehow they did.

I was waiting on Aisha, Destiny's partner to find out who them niggas was and what all they said so that I could be ready. I wasn't trying to leave my family behind, so I was trying to make sure I did what I had to do to stay a free man. I had only told Emon and Dae what I felt they needed to know, because I knew they would only want some action. I was trying to keep them niggas free and safe, but I knew not to expect anything less than the reaction I got from them.

I kissed Cuba up and down her back and then her neck before I rubbing my hand up the front of her night gown, grabbing her breast into my hand. I knew she wasn't comfortable with having sex with me just yet, and I could understand that, but no lie, a nigga hadn't had any since before all this shit happened. Now that I was laying next to my wife, I was ready to explode. I pulled Cuba's head back and forced her to look up at me. Her eyes fluttered open, and I kissed her on her lips before sliding my tongue into her mouth.

"Hmmm," she moaned making my dick get harder. My shit was thumping like a muthafucka in my boxers, and I was trying my hardest to respect what Cuba wanted and give her time.

"How you gonna fall asleep on me?" I asked her, and she chuckled a little before closing her eyes back. I kissed her again, before I reached down and tried to slide her panties off. She grabbed my hand and tried to stop me, but I tugged and tugged at them before they were at her knees.

"Khi...,"Cuba said, and I cut her off by sliding my tongue into her mouth.

"I need you in the worst way baby," I told her. She moaned as I ran my fingers across her clit and began to massage it with my thumb. I pushed her panties down further and pulled her legs open wider. I moved my kisses down to her neck and then lifted up so that Cuba could lay back on the bed. Raising her gown up, I sucked her left breast into my mouth while slowly massaging between her legs.

"Shit...Khi, wait. I don't know if I'm ready," Cuba said as a tear slipped from her eye. I pulled her panties away and then removed my boxers. I climbed between her legs and then used my thumb to wipe the tears from her face.

"I'll go slow...be gentle and you just tell me if you need me to stop, but I need you right now. I wanna make love to you so bad. I need to feel you," I told Cuba, and she shut her eyes tightly before she looked up at me and looked into my eyes. When she relaxed, I placed the head of my dick at the entry of her pussy and shook my head. I was so fuckin' horny that I knew it would only take me a couple of minutes before I was nutting. I chuckled and Cuba's brows furrowed and she frowned.

"What's funny?" Cuba asked and I kissed her lips.

"Cause I'm a cum quick as hell."

"Maybe right now, that's a good thing...until you know...," Cuba said, and I nodded before I kissed her again and slowly slid inside of her. I sat there for a moment and just looked down at my wife. I often teased her about being ugly, but that was far from the truth. She was the most beautiful woman I had laid eyes on. I knew that when I first met her in Wal-Mart that she was the one for me. Every time I looked into her eyes, I knew that she was the woman I was gonna spend my life with. That's why, no matter what, I would never give up on us. Cuba had me doing shit that I would never do for another chick. I chased after her, because I knew her worth, and I knew what she meant to me, and hell, my daughter. Keeping Skylarr away from her was wrong as fuck, but I was desperate and wanted my damn wife back.

"Szzzz," Cuba sighed and started to tense up. I kissed her lips and gave her slow strokes until she got adjusted to my size again.

"Shit," I groaned and took one of Cuba's leg and wrapped it around my waist. Damn I was gonna be sick as fuck if I didn't beat whatever the FEDs had coming for me. Knowing I was gonna have to leave this behind had me feeling sick to my stomach. The separation may have been a good thing, because I was appreciating every minute of this and knew that I would never make the mistake of fucking it up again.

"Khi," Cuba moaned. She tossed her head back, and I took my tongue and licked up the center of her neck. I tried my hardest to go as slow as possible, but it seemed like that only made Cuba get wetter and wetter. I grabbed her other leg and pulled it over the other side of my waist and just went the fuck in. Cuba gushed all over my dick and she squeezed her muscles together trying to clasp me in place. Her pussy's grip had my dick thumping hard as fuck, and I tried to pull back so that I wouldn't cum so fast, but Cuba wasn't having that. She tossed her hips into mine a few times before she was raining down on my dick and moaning loudly in pleasure.

"I'm cumming! Damn it, Khi," Cuba cried out, and my ass had to tap the fuck out on this one. I spilled my seeds inside of her, slowly stroking in and out of her until I was completely drained.

"Told you that shit was gonna be quick," I said, and for some reason, I became irritated as fuck. I rolled over onto my back and stared up at the ceiling while Cuba climbed out of bed and walked into the bathroom. I didn't even wait for her to come back before I got up and grabbed my sweats and the keys to my car. Walking outside of the house, I looked up to see that the sun was rising and the niggas that I had on Cuba's house was standing out front air boxing with one another. I nodded at them, then opened the door to my car and reached inside and pulled out a baggie of weed and a couple of cigars.

I thought that, when I finally bust a good nut, I was gonna be relaxed, but my irritation level was high as fuck. I slammed the door to my car and walked back inside of the house, first going to check on my daughter before I walked back into Cuba's room. She was standing butt ass naked in front of the dresser, going through one of her drawers. I shook my head at the scar on her back and hurried to roll my fuckin' blunt. Knowing that the nigga Chaison had been inside of Cuba had me heated like a muthafucka. I was madder now than I had been earlier.

"Where you about to go?" I asked Cuba and frowned. She pulled out a matching bra and panties set and walked over to her closet coming out with some business clothes. I raised my brow before I walked over to the trash and emptied the tobacco from the cigar inside and then went to sit down on the bed.

"I told you, I have to go to work," Cuba answered, and I snatched the clothes out of her hand and tossed the shit on the floor.

"Didn't I tell you I wanted to spend the day with you? Get your assistant to take care of shit today. Besides, I need you to come with me so I can put all this shit in your name," I told Cuba, and she looked at me with a frown on her face.

"Damn, it didn't take long for you to go back to your old ass ways. You didn't have to snatch that out my hand like that."

"We got shit to do, and I don't know if I really want you going back to that office unless I'm right there with you."

"What?"

"You heard me. Matter of fact, maybe you should just work out the house. It's big enough for you to do what you gotta do at the house."

"No...it's not. My potential clients come in and look at the samples of the work I have done."

"Can't you just send them pics through email or something?" I asked her, and Cuba shook her head and walked away. "Yes the fuck you can."

"No, I can't, and I'm not going to that house," Cuba said just as I lit the tip of my blunt. She was inside of the bathroom and had turned on the water so I was trying to make sure I had heard her clearly. I took a pull from the blunt and walked inside of the bathroom.

"Say what?"

"I'm not going to that house."

"What you mean?" I asked and frowned.

"I think that we need to make sure that this is gonna work out before I just up and leave my damn house."

"Make sure this gonna work out. Why the fuck wouldn't it work out, Cuba?"

"Look how you acting now! You was just begging me for another chance and now you cussing at me and controlling what I do. You told me you didn't have a problem with me working and making my own money, now you want me to be at home," Cuba said and sighed. She turned on the water to the faucet and grabbed her toothbrush and toothpaste.

"I never said you couldn't work, Cuba, I said that you should work from the house. But you pissing me the fuck off talking about you ain't coming home. The fuck you mean? And where is your fuckin' ring."

"Khi...just leave!" Cuba yelled. She turned around and pushed me and I gritted down my bottom lip before sucking my teeth and staring down at her. "Leave!"

I took a pull off the blunt and then blew smoke in the air while still keeping my eyes on Cuba. Before I knew it, I had turned around and punched a big ass hole in the wall followed by kicking the muthafuka over and over again until it was a hole big enough for me to crawl through. I rushed out of the bathroom refusing to look back at Cuba, because I knew that she was crying. Maybe her not telling me in the beginning was a good thing, because now that I knew, I had no idea how I was gonna handle this shit.

"Daddy!" I heard Skylarr call out, but I was seeing nothing but red and kept going. I damn near tore the door down trying to get out of that house and out to my car. Once inside, I placed the keys in the ignition, cranked the car, and peeled the fuck off. The only thing that was gonna make me feel better at this point was finding them niggas that was snitching and making them pay for ever opening up their mouths.

9

TANGIE

1 week later...

It had been eight days since I had given birth to my first child Cassidy Jr, and even though Cassidy hadn't been with me in the delivery room, he hadn't left my side since he showed up at the hospital. He was helping me adjust to motherhood and was going through every little feeding and diaper change with me. Any time he saw that I was too tired or in too much pain from my C-Section scar, he would grab CJ out of my crib, change his diaper, and then place him on my breast while still allowing me to sleep. Cassidy was a God send for real. He told me that he was gonna do everything in his power to make it up to me and he had tenfold. I didn't have any complaints.

Although, I was mad as fuck that he'd been arrested, I knew that it wasn't something that he had done on purpose, so I stopped making him feel bad about it. I made sure that he knew that I was thankful for everything that he did big or small. That was one thing that I had learned through our counseling sessions was that Cass hated to not feel wanted or even unappreciated. He said that was what made him shut out and cheat on me. He loved to feel needed and like he was doing something right instead of me always chastising him and pointing out every little thing that he did wrong, so I tried to make sure that I let him know as often as possible that he was loved by me and the kids, and that he was more than appreciated.

Today was the first day that Cass was stepping out and getting back in the streets, and I wasn't happy about it, but it was what I signed up for by fucking with a dope boy. He had long ago neglected his brothers even after finding out that, somehow the FEDs were now involved with a package, and that Khi was planning to take full responsibility for it. I could tell that it was eating away at him that he couldn't be there for them, especially for Khi, which was why, last night, I told him that he needed to just go. He was quiet all the time and super moody whenever I said something to him. I'd rather he did what he needed to do so that he wouldn't blame me in case something bad happened, God forbid.

"A'ight, you need me to get anything before I head out," Cassidy asked as he emerged from the bathroom. I looked at him dressed in a black Balmain's shirt, and a pair of crisp white Balmain jeans. His hair was wild and curly being that he'd just washed it, and I shook my head cause I hated it like that, but my situation made it hard for me to sit up long enough for me to braid him up so I couldn't say too much about it.

"Nah, I'm good. Cuba is bringing Skylarr and BJ by in about an hour, and they're supposed to spend the day with me so I should be okay," I told Cassidy, and he walked over to me and kissed me on my lips.

"I want some," Cassidy said while looking down at me.

"Hell no." I laughed, shook my head, and then quickly pushed his hand away when he tried to rub between my legs. He knew damn well I had to wait six weeks before having sex again.

"Shit, why not. You ain't gotta do nothing but lay there. It ain't like that big ass nigga came out your pussy so you should be good down there."

"Cassidy, no. Damn, at least give my damn stitches time to heal before we try anything. I'm fresh out of surgery and you trying to send me to the hospital again."

"Hell yea, with another baby in your stomach," Cassidy laughed, and I looked at him like he was crazy. "Sit up for me."

"Okay," I said and grabbed a hold of Cassidy's arm to pull myself up. The pain wasn't as bad as it was the first few days that I'd come home, but it was still pretty rough. I had to walk kneeled over and could really only stay on my feet long enough to take a quick shower, pick CJ up, and then lay my ass right back down.

Cassidy kneeled down in front of me and pulled my hands into his. I looked at him strangely, because his hands were shaking and he wouldn't even look up at me. Knowing that the police could come back at any time and hit him with murder charges kept the both of us on edge. He promised that he would keep me informed with everything that was going on, and I just hoped that he wasn't about to hit me with some bad news right now. I sighed and forced Cassidy to look up at me. I pushed his hair back away from his face and stared at him.

"I love you...you know that right?" Cassidy said and sighed.

"Yes, and I love you, too," I told him, and he nodded.

"How much do you love me?"

"Enough that I know that I'm afraid to live without you again."

"You won't have to. I'mma make sure of that, but even then, I need you to ride for me, Tangie. Shit is gonna get rocky...tough, and I need to know you got my back through all of this shit. Everything."

"I do, Cass. I want this to work between us and for us to be a family. I know we still got a lot of shit to work on, but I know we gonna be good," I said to Cassidy and watched as he went into his pocket and came out with a box.

My hands immediately went up to my face, and I covered my mouth in shock as Cassidy opened the box to the biggest damn diamond ring I had ever seen in my life. Tears immediately fell from my eyes, and I started shaking my head not believing that this was happening. I really loved Cassidy...had always loved this man. He was my first everything and anything between that was just a way to cover up the wounds that I had from losing him. He had hurt me in the past and had shown me that he was willing to right his wrongs for the sake of our relationship.

"You know I'm not real big on words and shit, but I do love you. Ever since I first met you, I knew that you was gonna one day be my wife. That bid was hard as fuck, because I didn't have my lady riding with me. When I got locked up, I learned that a man should never take advantage of a queen when he finds her. I know I've had some fuck-ups along the way, and I'm trying to make sure that I never make the same mistake twice to show you that I can be the man you need me to be. Anyway, I just wanna know if I got you for life shawty, can you...will you be my wife?" Cassidy asked, and I nodded yes. Tears were pouring so fast from my eyes, and I was so hysterical, that I could barely even talk.

"Yes," I mumbled, as I wiped the tears away.

Cassidy smiled as he slid the rock onto my finger and then gently pulled me up from the bed and into his arms. I hugged him so tightly and cried on his shoulder before I found my way to his lips and kissed them. Sliding my tongue into his mouth, I made love to his tongue and could feel Cassidy's hand going to places that they shouldn't go. I was so caught up in the moment that I didn't even stop him. He laid me back on the bed and pulled my underwear down my legs and tossed them to the side. I shook my head and watched as he allowed his pants to drop to his ankles and then as he pulled his briefs down. Gently, Cassidy climbed on top of me and slowly slid himself inside of me.

"You good," Cassidy asked, and I shook my head yes. I couldn't believe that we were doing this so soon, but the moment just felt so right. I closed my eyes and wrapped my arms around Cassidy. He slid in and out of me before pulling my gown over my head and kissing all over my body. He brought my nipple up to his mouth, and we had to both laugh when he pulled back remembering that I now had a supply of milk inside of my breasts. Instead of sucking on my nipples though, he licked around them and started pumping faster. I couldn't help it as I slowly brought my legs up to wrap around Cass' waist. I thought I was gonna be in pain down there or that it might not feel good, but it felt just as good as it always had, and I was getting ready to cum.

"Mmmmh, baby!" I cried out and gently threw my hips into Cass'. I knew that I was gonna pay for this shit later, but right now, I didn't care. Cass felt so damn good, and I was happy to see that he was enjoying it as well. He was biting down on his lip, and I knew that was because he hated when he moaned.

"Aahhh," Cass groaned and started stroking in and out of me faster and faster. He shook his head and said fuck it and sucked my nipple into his mouth. I could feel his dick growing harder the closer I came to climaxing. Long and deep, Cassidy dug inside of me causing me to scream out in ecstasy.

"Fuck, Cassidy, I'm cumming so damn hard right now. Shit it hurts, but feels so damn good."

"I'm about to cum too. Shit, I'm about to cum, Tangie...arghhh!" Cassidy yelled, and before I could even protest and tell his ass to pull out, he hit me with one, long, powerful stroke that stunned me into silence while spilling every bit of himself inside of me. He crashed on top of me while placing small kisses on the side of my face. "Damn, that shit felt so good. Shit bae, how the fuck I'm supposed to wait now after this."

"Damn it, Cass, get up. You know I don't have any birth control yet. What if I get pregnant?"

"So what? You about to be my wife, fuck does it matter?" Cassidy ignorantly said and rolled off of me. "Be still, let me grab you and towel, and I'm a go get that ice pack out the freezer for your stomach."

I reached under my pillow as soon as Cassidy walked off ready to grab my phone to text Cuba. I was about to ask her to stop and grab me a Plan-B from the pharmacy when out of the corner of my eye I saw Cassie standing in the doorway rubbing her eyes. I quickly grabbed for the blanket to cover myself with when she came further into the room.

"My eye hurts," Cassie whined as she continued to rub her eye.

She brought her hand down, and that was when I noticed something sitting on her cheek.

"What the hell is that on your eye?" I asked just as Cassidy stepped back into the room.

"It hurts," she whined, and I frowned once she looked up at me with two brown eyes.

"Is that a fuckin' contact?"

10

CUBA

I walked inside of the empty restaurant hand in hand with Khi. He was dressed in a Gucci custom-fitted suit with a pair of suede Gucci loafers. This was the nicest I had seen him look in a very long time. Our separation had killed his spirits, which in turn had caused him to no longer give a fuck about the way he looked.

Over the course of a week, we had gotten back together, broken up, and just a couple of days ago, got back together again. It was just a weird and stressful situation. Khi would come to me crying about how he wasn't gonna fuck up again and how much he loved me, and as soon as I gave in to him and had sex with him, he was flipping the fuck out on me.

A few days ago, he called me an evil, conniving bitch, and told me that, if I ever killed another one of his kids, he was going to take me out the same way he had done Briana. I cried so hard in front of him after he had said it, then he walked away from me like I wasn't shit only to come back the next day saying that he was drunk and didn't mean any of it.

I knew that drinking and sipping that damn lean lately had been a big part of Khi's new everyday life, but I had hoped that he wasn't gonna make a continuous habit out of it. He complained before about how irrational lean had made Dae and how it was a big part of the reason why the choices he made in the past were so damn foolish. Now, here he was doing the same thing.

He was pressuring and pressuring me to come to the house that he had bought for us before the separation, but we needed to sit down and have a serious talk about everything that was going on. I wanted to be with Khi, work on my marriage, and fix all the problems that we had now so that in the future our union was filled with nothing but bliss, but Khi was really making me mad that I didn't stick to my guns and just leave this shit alone.

He was different. His attitude wasn't the same...I mean, Khi had always been dominant, like the alpha male kind of shit, and it was something I had to get used to since Rue was nothing like it. I didn't mind it one bit, but there was a difference in leading your lady and being flat-out disrespectful. Khi had crossed that line too many times in just this past week alone, and the only reason why I was here with him tonight was because he begged me to come. He said that he needed everyone that he loved to be here tonight, because he had a huge announcement to make.

All I knew is that all week, he'd prohibited me from going to work at my business just so that I could sign all types of paperwork. We had met with his lawyer a few times, and he'd made sure that I went and set up bank accounts for all the kids in their names.

I asked him if this had anything to do with the FEDs, and the fact that someone had snitched on him, and all he said was that everything was going to be cool, and that he was just taking steps to have things in place in case the worse did happen. No lie, no matter how much he was getting on my damn nerves, I don't know what I would do if Khi went to jail.

Tangie told me about how sick she was when she'd found out that Cass was gonna have to do a bid, and being that I had gone to prison myself, I knew how fuckin' hard that shit was. I didn't wanna go through that at all.

"That's why I told you not to wear that dress. Seems like every time you take a step, it gets shorter and shorter," Khi said to me as we made our way towards the back of the restaurant where everyone was sitting. I rolled my eyes and looked at my dress. It was probably a little smaller now being that I had put on a few pounds, but it wasn't that damn bad. Khi was just looking for something to pick at me about to find another reason why I needed to be at home so that he could watch me more closely. I halfway believed he thought I cheated or was cheating on him based off the way he was acting.

It was crazy cause he hadn't started acting this way until I accidentally spilled that I had been raped by that fuck nigga, Chaison. Khi claimed that it didn't bother him, but it was funny how after sex, there was a problem. I picked up on it after the third time we made love, and the next time he tried, I pushed him away and told him I wasn't feeling good, but Khi swore up and down his dick always made shit better. I thought by me telling him what happened it would make him never want to touch me again, but Khi seemed to want me just as much as before. It was just the part after that was the problem.

"I'll be sure I sit down the entire time, Khi," I said just before we made it to the table. The first person that I spotted was Emon, and that was because he had his eyes planted on me. I hurried up and looked away from him and to the girl that he had sitting next to him. She was a pretty little mixed chick that looked like she was no older than about nineteen or twenty years old. She had her hair pulled up into a ponytail with Chinese cut bangs that fell just above her eyes. She was cute, but I could already tell that they wouldn't last.

"Sit down, babe," Khi said after catching my attention. He pulled my chair out and I sat down in my seat. Across from me was Cassidy, and I knew that Tangie wasn't able to make it. After visiting with her and my little cousin on yesterday, it made me really regret aborting my baby. I don't know what the hell I was thinking, and I just hoped that one day, God would allow me to right my wrong. I wasn't quite ready right now being that shit with me and Khi was rocky, but when things did get back on track, I wanted to give him the child that we both really wanted.

After a few minutes of everyone getting settled in, Khi stood to his feet and cleared his throat. He loosened the top of his tie and then looked around at everyone. We were at a steak house in Downtown Dallas called Dakota's, and Khi had the entire restaurant shut down so that we can be alone for whatever it was that he had to tell us.

"Preciate everybody for being here. I kinda just wanted to get my family together in one room so that we can relax and have some drinks while I made this little announcement. Y'all know the shit that popped off with the FEDs and shit...I didn't tell you Cass, Emon, or Dae that them niggas did snitch on a nigga, and yesterday morning, KaeDee found out that an indictment is coming my way pretty soon."

"What?" Emon said catching my attention. I frowned as a huge lump formed in my throat. I knew I wasn't hearing this correctly. Khi was just saying that it was a possibility, but now it was sounding like he was positive that he was going to jail. My heart thumped so loud and hard against my chest that it took everything in me not to cry.

"What that mean? An indictment?" Dae asked, and I buried my head into my hands.

"Meaning they already got a grand jury to say there was enough evidence to file charges against me."

"According to what? You wasn't even there! How they gonna charge you with some shit and you wasn't even there? This don't even sound right to me, bruh! And I thought you was gonna have some names days ago. We could've been rode out on them niggas man, for real. This shit ain't even right, bruh," Dae said, and I couldn't hold back any longer.

I started crying uncontrollably causing Khi to pull me up from my chair and wrap his arms around me. I buried my head into his chest mad that I didn't make up with him months ago. All that time I spent away from him was time that could've been spent together.

"Aisha wasn't able to get the names, because they threw the niggas in protective custody before she could. She's working on it, but only certain ranks can find out where they are. Truthfully, she might never find out until it's time to go trial."

"But KaeDee gonna handle everything, and he's gonna make sure you're straight, right?" Cassidy asked, and I took in a few deep breaths to try and get myself together. I wanted to know the answer to that question too. I mean, he was the lawyer of the family, and this was what he was there for. This was the reason that they had removed him from the streets and made sure he really never got his hands dirty. He was supposed to protect them from the law, and I prayed to God that he could save Khi.

"I should have information on the indictment on my desk by the morning, and I will know exactly what I'm dealing with, but I'm gonna do everything to make sure that you and Khi both stay out prison. We can't lose no one else to the chain gang. That's been our life since we been kids, and I'm sick of this shit. We gotta move different and make smarter decisions. This right here...never again, Emon," KaeDee said pointing to Emon's girlfriend.

"What you mean?" Emon asked and furrowed his brow.

"Nigga, Khi said family, and she ain't family," KaeDee told him, and Khi kissed me on the neck and guided me to sit back down.

"Yasline is my girl, though...," Emon called out.

"And that's fine, but until she's your wife, never bring her to something so personal again," KaeDee told him, and Emon sucked his teeth and grabbed Yasline's hand. He forcefully stood up from the table causing his chair to fall onto the floor behind him.

"I'm out," Emon said and yanked Yasline so hard by her arm that she almost tripped over her heels and fell to the floor. Her hips rocked hard from side to side as she did her best to keep up with Emon. Khi looked behind them, and I could see that he was upset by the way that his jaw was twitching and how hard he clung onto the pockets to his pants. He didn't say anything; he just let Emon go.

I looked over at Dae and could see that he was going crazy with the news that Khi had given to us. He'd made a complete turnaround, but I still didn't like his ass. We communicated as less as possible, unless it had something to do with my nephew. He would try to hold a conversation with me, but I never had none back to give his ass. That was Khi and BJ's family, but he would never be mine. I rolled my eyes and looked up at Khi who was looking real agitated right now.

"You wanna leave?" I asked, as I tugged at the arm of his jacket; he looked down at me and nodded his head yes.

"Go to the car and let me talk to these niggas for a minute," Khi said tight-lipped, and I nodded, grabbed his keys when he handed them to me, and made my way out to his car. Mario was waiting nearby, and he quickly ran to the passenger's side door and pulled it open, and I sat down inside and closed the door behind me.

After waiting a few minutes, I reached for the stereo to turn to some music when my phone vibrated in my pocketbook. When I pulled it out, I saw Emon's number flash across the screen, and the message that he'd sent made my heart skip a beat.

Emon: You could've told me you was gonna let that nigga know what happened. Do you plan on telling him everything? Thought we made a promise...smh

I looked up to see Khi coming through the parking lot, and I quickly unlocked my phone to delete the text message that Emon had sent to me. I let out a long, exhausting breath before sliding my phone into my purse. Damn I would be glad when I could just live a stress-free and normal life, and I was starting to think that that would only happen after death.

I had been cursed. It seemed like the moment I stepped out of my parents' home thinking I was grown and could handle the world on my own, boy was I wrong. It seemed like everything that my parents warned me of was happening left and right, and there was no escaping it.

"That ain't go nowhere near how I expected it would," Khi said and cranked up his car. He peeled out of the parking lot while loosening his tie a bit. He turned the volume up on the stereo to the max and leaned back in his seat while cruising down the freeway. I wanted to say something, but I knew that he wanted to be alone in his thoughts, so instead, I reached over and grabbed his free hand. He looked down at our hands joined together and then up at me. I gave him a light smile and then rested my head against the headrest.

It took us so long to get to where we were going that I didn't even realize that I had fallen asleep in the car until we had come to a stop. I looked around and noticed that we were at the house that Khi had bought for us before the separation. I had completely forgotten how big and beautiful it was, and my eyes lit up instantly remembering how happy and how much joy I felt when we picked it out. Times like those were the times I cherished and wished that I could have more of.

"Where is Sky going to be tonight?" I asked Khi, and he climbed out of the car and walked around to open the door for me. He grabbed my hand and helped me out of the car, and we made our way inside. I looked around remembering a few of the details and had quickly noticed that Khi had completely furnished the entire place.

"Figured we can enjoy our time here together for as long as possible before they come and take it away," Khi said, solemnly, and I looked up at him.

"What do you mean? Take what away?" I asked him, and he completely removed his tie and jacket and tossed it on the table that sat in the foyer of the home.

"You know, if the FEDs suspect anything was bought with illegal money, they seize it all. Everything that's in my name, they gonna take it. I couldn't put this house in your name, because it's too far outside of your income bracket, and I didn't want them fucking with you. That's why I only did the place you at now. The two cars are yours, and you know I got the little accounts set up for the kids. Tomorrow, we going back down to speak with the lawyers, and they gonna draw up a separation agreement dated back a few months ago to say that we wasn't together when this shit came down. I don't want them coming to you for shit."

"Wow, do you think you're gonna get locked up, Khi?"

"Yea, I'mma keep it one hundred with you. I'm gonna have to do some time; I just don't know how much yet. Ain't no escaping a FED case, bae. When they come for you, it's cause they got everything they need to convict you."

"It gotta be something we can do though. This just don't sound right, Khi."

"Yea, it don't, but I'm doing what I can. In the meantime, we just need to enjoy the time we do have, because one day it's gonna be cut short. Come here," Khi said and held his hand out for me. I walked over to him, and he took my hand into his and led me up the stairs. We went inside of the master bedroom and then into the bathroom.

Khi walked over to the big whirlpool Jacuzzi tub and turned the water onto high. He sat on the edge of the tub and pulled me in front of him. First, he reached under my dress, and when he noticed I didn't have any panties on, he looked up at me and sucked his teeth.

"Really?" he asked and I shrugged.

"What?" I asked like I had no idea what he was talking about.

"This what you gonna be doing when I'm gone. Walking around in little ass dresses with no panties on."

"Thought you liked it when I didn't wear any panties. I'm not cheating on you, Khi," I told him, and he frowned.

"I never said you was."

"Yea, but you acting as if I am...or are you really having a hard time accepting the fact that I was raped," I said becoming agitated and now uncomfortable in front of Khi. I pulled away from him, and he pulled me back and wrapped his arms around my waist.

"Why wouldn't I be uncomfortable? Every time I make love to you, I think about Chaison and the shit he did and how I couldn't stop it from happening. I love the way your pussy feel baby, and knowing that a nigga got a piece of what was mine without fuckin' permission burns me up inside. I really wanna go and dig that nigga up from where the fuck we buried his ass and torture him until I feel better. I'm not uncomfortable because of anything that has to do with you...just an ego thing."

"Is that why you've been snapping on me every time afterwards?" I asked and Khi nodded.

"Maybe...I don't know. So much going on right now. I don't know what the fuck is wrong with me. I feel like I'm losing myself every day. I been drinking more and more, finishing an ounce of syrup a day, and I know it's only a matter of time before shit goes haywire. When it does, just know that it was nothing you ever did. I love you, Cuba. Just know that."

"I know that you do, and I did want to talk to you about your syrup use. It's getting out of control, babe. I think that, if you stopped, you probably could get more of a handle on how you're feeling and how to deal with it."

Khi nodded but didn't say anything. He gently moved me out of the way before getting up and walking out of the bathroom. After a few minutes, he walked back inside butt naked with a blunt hanging from the tip of his lip. I chuckled and climbed out of my clothes as well. The water had damn near filled to the top, so Khi helped me climb up the two steps and guided me until I was comfortably inside. He sat across from me and relaxed his head against the built-in head-rest, while I made my way over to him and pulled the blunt from his mouth, placing it inside of mine.

"I think I know a way that you can find out who the guys are that's in protective custody," I said, and Khi looked at me and frowned.

"Fuck is you talking about?" Khi asked, as I blew out a cloud of smoke.

"Send in someone and tell them to tell the FEDs that they have some information on you, but before they can give it up, they need to be placed into protective custody. This girl I was locked up with told me she had done the same thing when her boyfriend got knocked for drug trafficking, but she did it because she really thought she needed protection from him.

She said they took her to this halfway house in another city, and come to find out, there were two other people there that was snitching on her boyfriend. In order to get back in good with her boyfriend, she told him who the snitches was, and he killed them. I remember her telling me that she was surprised that they put her in the same place as the other ones, but the government be so damn broke, and it ain't like nothing you see on TV."

"I don't know about all that. Hell, it sounds like some shit that you see on TV. I think Aisha gonna come through. She just gotta get the passwords and shit from one of the niggas she works with, and she told me to give her a week. It's been about five days, so I'm waiting. If that don't come through, then, I'll try something else. It's cool...long as I got the shit taken care of before I go to trial, then I ain't gonna too much worry about it. For now, I just want you to come home, get my daughter, and for us to be a fuckin' family like we supposed to be."

"You gon' stop sipping on that damn syrup," I asked Khi as I looked into his eyes and wrapped my arms around his neck. I kissed him on the lips and then pulled back to look at him again.

"I'll do whatever you want me to do if it means you coming home."

"Okay...I'll come," I told him, and he bit down on his bottom lip. I placed the blunt back inside of his mouth, and he took a pull from it before sitting it on the side of the tub. I didn't know what was gonna happen with Khi, but I was hoping that, in the end, he could beat this shit and not end up behind bars. He was right, though; we did need to be a family, and we did need to enjoy our time together. Time was something that was never on a person's side, so I wanted to make sure that I spent every minute that I could with Khi. We had a lot of catching up to do.

11

EMON

"I need to talk to you," Yasline said to me, and I looked at her and frowned.

"Don't you see me talking right now," I said to her and brought my attention back to my homie AP and his little brother Juan. These were the same two niggas that I got knocked by twelve with the night after I put a bullet in that pussy Amrin. I bodied that nigga off the simple fact that he tried to play me like I was some hoe in front of my niggas. He came at me talking about the weed I robbed his bitch ass daddy for was his and that if I didn't give it back to him, he was gonna murder me. I had to laugh that shit off, and then something in me just snapped. I guess it was the fact that the words that Clarke told me before I pistol whipped his ass played in my head over and over again like a nigga's favorite song.

"You look just like my youngest son. You and Amrin are only eleven months apart, and I swear you look just like him. I'm your father, son. Did your mother ever tell you about me?"

Seeing that nigga Amrin up close had me feeling like Clarke might have been telling the truth. I knew that I really didn't favor my brothers too much. I had some of my mother's features which had me looking a little like Dae's ass more than anything, but me and that nigga Amrin could pass for twins. I was so fucked up in the head that I didn't even think clearly when I put a bullet in his head. I didn't know that nigga nor his bitch ass daddy.

As far as I knew, I was a Prince. I admired the fuck out of my daddy—or the nigga I thought was my daddy. Not only that, the bond I had with my brothers was A-1, and at the time, I was trying to keep what I thought was a secret a secret. I had no idea that my pops already knew that I wasn't his real child and that Khi did too. That was the reason I was so fuckin' mad when I came home; Khi knew all along and never told me shit.

I quickly hit his ass with that fye. To me, it was nothing, but later I had found out that Amrin really might have been my brother. I had got a letter from that nigga Chaison saying that we shared the same father and that Amrin was his little brother. I ain't even wanna believe it, but the only reason why I robbed Clarke that night and took that dope was because he claimed that I was possibly his son and that he had been trying to get to know me. They had me walking around all along thinking that I was something that I wasn't, and that shit hurt like hell.

"Nigga, you better take your ass in there and talk to your damn girl before she come out here and bust your shit," AP said to me, and I looked over at Yasline as she stood in the doorway of my townhouse with both hands on her hip staring at me.

"Chmmp, man a'ight. I'mma just get at you niggas later. Me and Dae supposed to be hitting the road in the morning, so I'll see y'all when I touch back down in the city," I told AP and Juan and dapped them both up before I walked away.

I reached out to wrap my hands around Yasline when I made it to her, and she pushed me away and dropped my phone into my hands. I looked down at the screen and saw a series of messages from Cuba.

Cuba: I didn't tell him anything, but that Chaison raped me. He doesn't know what happened with me and you, and I want to keep it that way...

Cuba: He can never know that! He's already going crazy.

Cuba: With him possibly going to jail, we can't tell him.

Cuba: Sorry I should've told you I said something, but it slipped out and yea...

Cuba: Thanks for everything though Emon. I'll never forget it. <3

"The fuck I tell you about going through my phone?" I said and pushed past Yasline and stormed into the bedroom. I sucked my teeth and pulled my shirt away before tossing it to the floor.

"I knew when I saw the way that you looked at her earlier that you fucked her! Really, E, your brother's wife? How fuckin' low can you get?"

"Man, get out my damn ear with all that shit. It's not even what you think. Stop going through my shit. I swea' that's the shit that's gonna get your worsem ass replaced," I said to Yasline, and she started shaking her head and speaking in Spanish. I sighed and grabbed my phone then went into the bathroom and closed the door behind me.

The shit that happened with me and Cuba was just something that we felt like we ain't need to discuss. I was mad that she had even told Khi about her being raped, especially since I was willing to take that shit to the grave. It wasn't even about me but about the fact that Chaison had did some really fucked up shit to Cuba that wasn't even called for, and I felt bad that she even had to go through any of it. I wished that I could've stopped it, but Chaison had me tied down so good that I couldn't do shit. It had only happened a couple of times, and the one time that...

"Tell me the truth! Did you fuck her?" Yasline yelled, interrupting my thoughts. I turned the water to shower on and climbed out of my jeans and briefs.

"I just told you that I didn't! The fuck is wrong with you. Damn, I'm wit your ass damn near every night..."

"Yes nigga, damn near every night. So where the hell do you be when you're not here."

"Yas, your ass just wanna argue, and I don't have time for that shit. That's why I'm not here every night. You stay in my face about this bullshit every time I'm around; it makes me not want to be wit you."

"You don't wanna be with me?" Yasline asked her voice cracking. I ran my hands over my face and stepped inside of the shower closing the glass door behind me. "E, you don't wanna be with me?"

I could hear Yas, but I pretended as if I didn't. When I first came home, Yas was a great distraction and something good to keep my mind off all the bullshit. I tried to fall in love with her, but that jealousy shit was a turnoff to me, especially when I knew I wasn't doing shit wrong. Yea, there were other chicks, but that was in the beginning and that was before I told her that I would try this exclusive thing with her.

She had to understand that I had just come home from serving time in prison and being locked down in any kind of way was not some shit I was trying to do. She was persistent and she was one of the only chicks that stayed in touch with a nigga when I was locked up, so I felt it was only right, but it was like as soon as I did that shit, she turned into a complaining, whining, nagging bitch. She was always in my shit about some bitch. She stayed checking a nigga phone and always had her nose in my business. I wanted to go off on KaeDee earlier for telling me I couldn't have Yasline around, but after thinking about the shit for a minute, I realized he was right and quickly shot all them niggas a text apologizing and letting them know that it wouldn't happen again.

Yas' ass was nosey as fuck, and she was the type that, if she felt like I had done something wrong to her, she would try to do something to get back at me. I was new to the game, but I knew how a talkative, petty bitch could get you and your whole crew taken down, and I be damned if I went back to prison.

Now, I had to sit here and try to convince her immature ass that I didn't sleep with my brother's wife. I knew that if Yasline felt like I had, she wouldn't hesitate to go and ask Cuba for herself, and I ain't want that shit happening. I hopped out the shower after rinsing the soap off my body and reached for the towel that hung on the towel rack nearby. Wrapping it around the lower half of my body, I stood in front of the sink and took care of my hygiene before I walked past Yasline and into the bedroom. I laid back on the bed and rested my hands behind my head.

Yasline came and sat next to me, and I sighed before pulling her toward me and making her straddle me. Yasline was only twenty years old so some of her ways was to be expected, but if she was gonna be fuckin' with a nigga like me, she was gonna have to grow up. With Khi possibly going away, I knew I was gonna have to step in and help out more than ever no matter how many times they told me they didn't want me to.

They was all scared that I was gonna fuck up and do something stupid again, but my time behind bars had done me well. I was always reading some shit and stayed getting schooled by the OGs. I knew that had I been smarter and not some hothead back then that I would've never gotten locked up to begin with.

"When you gonna start trusting your man?" I said as I ran my hand under Yas' shirt and grabbed her titty. I bit down on my bottom lip and looked up at her.

"I'm sorry. You just be having me going crazy, E. I see how you were before we committed to each other, and I just be scared that you're still doing the same thing. I love you so much, bae."

"I told you that I ain't fucking around and with my brother's wife at that...come on, now, what kind of shit is that?"

"Then, tell me Papi, what was she talking about? What happened between the two of you?"

I sucked my teeth and swallowed back. I knew that I had to tell her ass something to get her to leave the shit alone, so I told her enough and only part of the truth. She didn't need to know shit else.

"I was in the same room when that shit happened to her...that's all. I saw some shit that I wish I didn't have to see. I couldn't stop it, and it makes me feel like a weak ass nigga for not being able to do nothing. Cuba knows that I saw her, and it's just awkward between us, so to not make shit weird for her and my brother's relationship, we promised each other that we wouldn't say nothing."

"Saw what? What did you see?" Yasline asked as she raised a brow and looked down at her. "You told me before that you saw him beating her and that when she tried to free you, he beat her worse and pushed her into the wall. Is that not what you're saying now?"

"I saw him rape her, a'ight? Leave the shit alone, Yas. Don't be going around talking about the shit with your messy ass homegirls either. The only reason why I'm telling you this because you refuse to believe that a nigga ain't doing your ass wrong. I look out for my peoples, and Cuba is my peoples. The same way I look out for her is the same way I would look out for you as long as you don't give me a reason not to."

"Oh, my God. That has to be so hard for the both of you. I'm so sorry, E, please forgive me."

"It's nothing. Don't ever bring that shit up again. Now, come here," I told Yasline, and she leaned over and kissed my lips. She reached behind her and found her way through the opening of my towel and wrapped her hand around my dick. She massaged it with her soft hands and slid her tongue into my mouth.

Yasline stood over me and pulled the dress she was wearing over her head and tossed it to the floor. She hadn't been wearing nothing underneath so she stood over me completely naked with a finger in her pussy. After massaging herself for a few seconds, she brought her finger up to her mouth, licked it, and then slowly slid down on my dick.

"Fuck," she hissed, as she planted both of her feet on the side of me and used them to bounce up and down.

"Ride that dick, Ma," I said, as I slapped her on the ass and then grabbed a handful of it. I guided her up and down on my stick and she cried out in pleasure while tossing her head back. Yasline had that good, and her shit stayed sloppy wet, but that wasn't enough for a nigga like me. For now, I was gonna keep her little ass around until I made something shake with somebody else. Every day she turned me off, it made me want to be turned on to something better. I should've listened to Khi when he told me that these half-Spanish, half-Black chicks was crazy. Every time that nigga either wrote me or came to see me when I was locked up, he had something to tell me about his baby mama Selena. She was a crazy ass chick that stayed in some drama, and I was starting to see the same with Yasline.

If I stared into her eyes long enough, like my mama used to say, then all I could see was darkness. She was a cold ass bitch that I knew would get me hemmed up if I didn't leave her alone. Besides, I wanted what Khi had. The way Cuba looked at him, and the way he looked at her was some of the dopest shit that I had ever seen, and that was exactly why I needed me a chic just like my sister-in-law.

12

CASSIDY

"Can't believe you got me down here doing this shit," I said to Tangie as I paced back and forth across the waiting room floor.

"You don't wanna know the truth, Cass?" Tangie asked and I looked at her and frowned.

"No...man damn," I said and sighed. I looked at Cassie in her natural state with her two regular brown eyes and wild and curly hair and didn't know what to think. I didn't know if it was because I was trying too hard or if she really still did look like a nigga. After she walked in the other day with the damn contact stuck to her face, Tangie freaked. She swore up and down that me and Jourdin had plotted against her and pretended like Cassie was mine just so me and her can fuck around. That was the dumbest shit I had ever heard, but when Tangie got something in her mind, it didn't matter what the fuck I said, she was gonna make it come true. Had me down here taking a DNA test for some shit that I already knew. I didn't give a fuck if Cassie was mine or not at this point. Hell, she became mine when I ended her mama's life. What the fuck did Tangie think I was gonna send her to her grandmother or let her go to foster care? This shit was fuckin' blew me. Muthafuckin' police constantly at my doorstep with more and more questions about Jourdin's death and Tangie thought this was a good idea. All I felt was that this was another way for them pussies to come after me and try to use this shit against me. They was waiting on me to make on wrong move so that they could stick me with them murder charges. Thinking about it made me antsy and I grabbed Cassie's hand and just left.

"Cass!" Tangie called after me, but I took my daughter and kept going. "Cassidy!"

"Where...where we going?" Cassie asked me and I looked down at her. She looked so much like my nieces and nephew that I had to wonder if it was a coincidence or if she really did have my blood running through her veins. Every morning she woke up and came running into my room, I always just stared at her while playing with her. I half-way wondered if Jourdin wasn't one-hundred percent sure if Cassie was mind and felt like she had to fuck with my daughter's eyes just in case that I wasn't.

"We gonna get you a Happy Meal and then we going home. What you think about that?"

"Yayyyy! Can I get two toys?" she said and held up two fingers in front of her face.

I laughed and nodded my head. Once we got to my car, I opened up the back door and helped Cassie get inside and into her carseat. By time I had buckled her in, Tangie had made it outside to the car and I walked over to her and helped her with CJ. I grabbed the car seat and strapped him in the back and then walked around and got inside of the car. When I started the engine, I looked over to notice Tangie's leg shaking uncontrollably so I knew that only meant that she was mad.

"Why did you walk out of there like that?" Tangie asked and I sighed as I pulled out of the parking lot.

"We'll talk about it later," I told her and she did a big ass dramatic sigh that made me snap.

"I said we'll fuckin' talk about it later! I should've never agreed to come down here and do this shit any damn way! Just to ease your muthafuckin' mind."

"You damn right! You and that bitch carried on a whole damn relationship while tossing me to the fuckin' side and I find out that she might not even be your damn child!"

"Man shut the fuck up! Shut the fuck up!" I roared and sped through the city's street, trying to get us home as quickly as possible.

"Don't tell me to shut up! You hurt me yet again, Cass, behind the same damn chick that helped lead to the loss of our first child and you want me to just sit back and take care of a child that might even be yours! How fair is that to me?"

"Shit is always about you. You don't give a fuck if them damn police bitches after me and looking for something to use against my ass. You just wanna do whatever it is you gotta do to make yourself feel better. Fuck you think I'm a do if she ain't mine? She still gonna stay with me. I'mma still be her fuckin' father and if you got a problem with that then bitch get the fuck on!" I yelled and gritted down on my teeth. I pulled the hair out of my face and looked through the rearview mirror at Cassie. Thankfully she wasn't really paying us any mind and I hoped that she didn't understand what the hell was going on.

"Really, Cass?" I'm a bitch now? That's how you feel after all you've done to me?"

"The fuck!" I sighed and reached over to turn the music up on the stereo. I tried to get lost in the music and drown Tangie out, but she was persistent on discussing this shit. Not giving a fuck if my daughter was in the damn backseat. Damn, we was talking about her and her mama—a couple of subjects I tried to be as sensitive as possible when it came to her. She missed her mama and I did my best to fill that void. I had hoped that Tangie would step in and do her all to make sure that Cassie never wanted for nothing or even had the opportunity to become sad over Jourdin not being around, but I could see that she was only doing the shit cause she felt like she had to and not because she wanted to.

"You've put me through so much shit, I swear I don't even know why I thought getting back with you was a good idea. Jourdin, Tameeka's ol worsem ass. That bitch stay threatening me behind your ass and you act like you just don't care. Got the nerve to say that everything is always about me. Not to mention that even after you cheated on me with that bitch, came home and sparked up a whole relationship with that broad, and I still accepted your child like she was my own."

"Yea and ready to get rid of her the minute you find out that she might not be mine after all. That's your muthafuckin' fault. Told your ass from day one that the kid wasn't mine, but you had to keep pushing the shit. Go find her Cass. Make sure that you don't have no kids running around here. Why else would Jourdin say she was yours if she isn't? Have you found your daughter yet? How about now, Cass?" I said mocking Tangie.

"Because I wanted to make sure you were gonna man up to your damn responsibilities."

"Do I look like I need your damn help to be a man? The fuck? I'm manning up to my responsibilities now. Her mama ain't here and she ain't never coming back. Either you gonna play that role or you gonna get the fuck on. The choice is yours."

"Just hurry up and take me home. I don't even know why I try with you, Cass. You are so fuckin' disrespectful."

"I'm disrespectful, but you the one think this shit was cool to discuss in front of my child after I told you we'll talk about it when we get home."

Finally, Tangie decided to dead the subject and kept her mouth closed on the rest of the ride to the house. As soon as we pulled up in front of the house, she hopped out of the car and snatched our son out of the car with an attitude. Instead of me going inside with her, I drove off and me and Cassie headed to the bruh's house. I knew that he had been trying his best to spend as much time with his family not knowing if he was gonna go to jail or not so I knew that he had my niece Skylarr with him. Cassie could use someone to play with and plus I wanted to know how he felt about the whole situation. Shit, I knew that I was wrong for just bringing Cassie into our home and lying to Tangie about Jourdin running off, but I did what I felt I had to do. Not only was I trying to protect myself, but I was trying to protect Cassie too. I knew that if Tangie even thought for one second that Cassie wasn't mine, she would want me to send her to live her great grandmother but I wasn't about to do that. That old woman could barely take care of herself let alone an active child like Cassie.

I pulled up to Khi's gate about twenty minutes later, an typed his gate code in. I nodded at the security before driving inside the iron gate when it opened up for me. I glared through the rear-view and noticed how Cassie perked up when she saw that we were coming in. I smirked knowing that she loved playing with her cousins. She was a couple of years older than Sky, but they loved playing with just about the same damn things—dolls and dress up.

"Come on," I told Cassie after I opened her door and allowed her to undo her own seatbelt. She hopped down out of her carseat and took off running towards Khi's house. When Cuba opened up the door, Cassie took off running inside without even speaking and I shook my head and chuckled. I nodded at Cuba and reached inside of the car to pull out a pre-rolled blunt. I grabbed a lighter and lit the tip of it before leaning up against the car.

A few minutes later, Khi emerged from the house dressed down in a pair of basketball shorts, a wife beater, and pair of Addidas flip flops. I choked back on the blunt and laughed when I noticed how chill he was. It was hardly ever a time I had seen him like this, shit not even when we was little niggas. Khi was always on a money making mission and never allowed himself to get too comfortable, but I guess when a nigga's life was hanging in the balance, it was either you stressed or you relaxed. I could only think that had I known back then that I was about to sit down and do that time, I probably would've done the same damn thing. Shit truthfully, it was some shit I thought about now, but things were always tense when I was around Tangie. One minute we were a happy couple and I knew there was no other place I wanted to be than with her, but days like this she made me rethink if I really wanted to commit the rest of my life to her.

"What up nigga?" Khi said and yawned. He dabbed me up and gave me a brief hug before he leaned against the car right next to me. I passed him the weed and sighed.

"You probably ain't even paid her no mind just now, but did you see Cassie?" I asked and he looked back and then at me and shook his head.

"I heard her run through the house calling Sky, but she ain't stop to speak to me. Little rude ass," Khi said and I chuckled.

"The whole shit with Jourdin was fucked up. The little bitch put a contact in Cassie's eye to make her look like me. Walked in on her the night before Emon got released and saw that shit. I snapped and beat the fuck outta o her until she died. I never said nothing to Tangie about it and just took Cassie home that night like nothing happened. The next day I went over to clean up everything and get rid of Jourdin, and I shot a text from Jourdin's phone to mine saying she was leaving and that she wanted me to take care of Cassie. I don't know...I snapped."

"Damn..."Khi said and shook his head. He pulled on the blunt before he passed it over to me.

"When the fuck was you gonna bring the rest of us up to date? You know KaeDee been doing everything he can to keep you from going down on shit and you kept acting like you ain't know what happened to Jourdin like we police or something."

"Wasn't even like that fam...was just trying to keep Tangie from finding out. I sit up and did the same shit Jourdin did and put that damn contact back in Cassie's eye. Fuckin' bought contact solution and all that trying to keep with the same damn lie cause I was scared Tangie was gonna leave me if she found out the truth. A few days ago though, Cassie walked in the room with the contact stuck to her face and I ain't no choice but to let be known that Jourdin lied."

"Damn, you told Tangie what you did to Jourdin?" Khi asked and I shook my head.

"Nah...cause she thinks me and Jourdin plotted against her and that was pretending that Cassie was mine just so we can keep fucking around."

"Bruh—Cassie looks just like you though my nigga. Just a little lighter skin complexion, but my nigga that's your seed," Khi said and I shook my head and tugged on the blunt.

"Yea that's exactly how I feel every time I look at her. I don't know what to do my nigga. I know for a fact that if she's not mine, Tangie wants me to send her to live with Jourdin's grandma, but I can't do that fam."

"Hell nah. She already know that you gotta raise the kid. Fuck she think this is? Tangie know better. Cassie gonna forever be a Prince baby no matter what. Tell sis to fall in line man."

"How the fuck do you do it nigga? Cuba and Tangie got the same damn blood and I swear half the time I can't stand being around that lady, bruh. I be thinking one day I'm about to be a happy married man to the lady I've always loved and then the next my nigga, I be like damn where the hoes at?" I said and Khi chuckled but as I was fuckin' for real.

"Cuba..." Khi sighed and looked toward his house. I could see the peace he had had him when he spoke about his wife. I was happy to see the two of them working through their problems because that nigga was sick as hell when she was telling that nigga she was done. I had never seen the bruh so out of pocket behind a shawty so I knew for a fact that the love was mad real. Normally, Khi would move the fuck around and on to the next chick, but with Cuba he never gave up.

"It's like one of them things that you just know. I knew for a fact that I was gonna settle down and marry her. When I first met her slick talking, nappy headed ass in Wal-Mart, I came outside excited as hell to tell the bruh that I had found the one. I didn't even know her name and she dissed the fuck out of me, but it was like my whole life flashed with her in those few minutes that I talked to her. All we gotta do is get that attitude in check and for her to understand who the fuck the boss and we good," Khi said an I nodded wondering if me and Tangie was doing the right thing. Sometimes I felt like I was forcing it with her because I wanted to be settled and because I knew that I loved her.

"Sometimes we can love somebody, but they not be the one for us. I loved Briana, but I knew she wasn't for me. Cuba...I just knew. I'll never second-guess that shit either. You change your mind too many times for you to be sure about if that's the woman you wanna marry bruh."

"Damn, I know, but how I am. Stubborn as fuck and be ready to say fuck it the minute I feel like something ain't for me. I don't wanna do Tangie like that because I really do love her, but it seems like no matter what, we just can't seem to get it right. Even with this counseling and these possible murder charges coming my way, I still don't feel no type of peace. Not the shit you got going here."

"Nigga everybody ain't gonna have the same thing I got here. How I found peace with shawty might not be the same way you have to find it with Tangie. It might take you two going through more shit than you've already been through. Shit look at what me and Cuba been through since I've met her...how many time she tried to leave a nigga."

"I hear you bruh, but everybody can see what you got here fam. Even that nigga Dae was just talking about the shit the other day with Emon. Nigga everybody want that Khia and Cuba relationship. Got a nigga out here hollering about relationship goals," I laughed and Khi chuckled as I passed him the blunt. "You hear anything about your case?"

"Yea, I gotta go turn myself in on the 15th. Aisha still ain't found out who them niggas is, but I talked to that nigga Tamar last night and he said he'll have the info for me in a couple of days. Nigga was mad I didn't come to him sooner, but hell I wasn't trying to come to him with this shit. Hell I don't even know how these niggas know about me."

"Right...yea let me know soon as you get them names bruh. We gonna fuck some shit up. Ain't nobody doing no more bids nigga, you hear me?" I said and slapped hands with Khi. I pulled him in for a hug and we stood outside of his house a little longer blazing and chopping it up about some of everything. I had never seen my brother in this state before and all I knew was that I wanted it. If we didn't find out who these niggas were, Khi could possibly do a long ass bid and he seemed to be taking the shit with ease and I knew that it was because of Cuba. She put his mind to rest and I wanted a chick that could the same for me. I loved the fuck out of Tangie, but I guess sometimes love wasn't enough.

13

CUBA

A week and a half later...

"Shit..." I said as I looked down at the two lines on the pregnancy test that said that I was pregnant. My hands trembled as I picked the test up from the bathroom cabinet and turned around only to run into Khi. He looked down at my shaking hands before grabbing the test from me and looking at it. I watched for his facial expression, but didn't see anything immediate. Dropping the test into the trash next, Khi walked over to the sink and washed his hands.

"I gotta go run to Houston for a couple of days and when I come back, we gonna talk about this a'ight?" Khi said and I nodded my head. It was six days before Khi had to turn himself in and the closer and closer we got to the date, the more and more we both seemed to be on edge. I knew that me being pregnant was something that the both of us wanted, but not at this moment. With Khi going to jail meant that I was gonna be home and pregnant alone to take care of Skylarr and the baby that I was pregnant with. I knew that was why he wasn't elated with joy at this moment. Khi was the kind of man that took care of his responsibilities and he was already having a hard time knowing that he was gonna have to leave me behind with Skylarr.

"Are you mad?" I asked him as he brushed his teeth. He shook his head no, but I couldn't help but notice how quiet he was being. "Do you want me to get an abortion?"

Khi looked at me through the mirror and if looks could kill, I would be dead right now. I ran my hands across my face and sighed. I only wanted to keep things easy for him. I knew this was hard for him. He was about to leave behind his family. Everybody relied on Khi for so much and in a matter of days, he was not gonna be around for any of us to call on. Just thinking about it caused me to get emotional. Out of nowhere, I broke down and started crying.

"Fuck," Khi said. He dropped his toothbrush in the sink and rushed over to me. He pulled me into his arms and took a set on the edge of the tub. I was trying so hard to hold it together, but the day just kept coming and it was like more and more news that we didn't need came along with the passing time. Cass had been charged with the murder of his baby mama and was now out on bail, but not allowed to leave the house. Dae and Emon were doing their best to run the family's drug business with Khi doing as much as he could without getting his hands dirty, but I could tell that it wasn't good enough for Khi.

"Kinda knew your ass was pregnant about a week ago, but I was hoping that you wasn't. Damn man," Khi said and I used the back of my hand to wipe the tears away. "This not how the fuck I wanted this shit to happen, Cuba. Ain't gonna be able to be here to see my fuckin' seed into this world and then you already having to take care of Skylarr. Shit."

"I'm sorry. I should've been more careful, but I wasn't taking anything because we wasn't together and then...it just all happened so fast and I wasn't even thinking about birth control," I said as more tears spilled from my eyes.

"It's cool baby...it's not your fault. I ain't mad that you pregnant. Just mad that I won't be here for you or the kid. You know it fucks with me that I don't get to see Kenya that damn much. I beg and beg Selena to let me see my damn child and she wanna be a bitch and keep my daughter from me. That shit really be eating a nigga up.

Kenya gonna grow up and not even know who the fuck I am. Soon as I was ready to take her to court behind this shit, these fucking charges come up. Can't win for losing."

Just as I was about to say something, Khi's phone started vibrating against the surface of the tub. He pulled it out of his pocket and looked at the screen. Whatever it was made him jump up from the tub and rush out of the room. I quickly followed behind him and watched as he ran to the closet and then came back out seconds later with two pistols in his hand. He tucked one behind him and then the other one, he put on his side.

"What's going on?" I asked him and he walked over to me and kissed me on the cheek and then on my lips. I looked up at him nervous and scared at what was about to happen. To see him grabbing pistols and running like this only meant that something was about to down.

"I'll be back. Do me a favor and stay inside today a'ight," Khi said and I nodded and followed behind him as he walked out of the room and walked down the stairs.

Soon as he was out of the door, one of his goonies stepped inside and looked at me and nodded their head. I walked away to go back inside of my bedroom and just climbed up in our bed. I rubbed my hand over my stomach and prayed that this baby would be okay. After losing one and then foolishly killing the other, I wanted so bad to have a baby with Khi. I knew that it wasn't the best time, but at least while Khi was gone, I would have something to hold onto that reminded me of him. Of course, I had Skylarr, but I wanted something that came from me and was also a part of him. I smiled at the thought of having a little boy that would come out looking just like him, how CJ came out looking just like his damn daddy. Thinking about the way CJ resembled Cassidy was so funny to me because all Tangie did was carry that boy. He looked nothing like her and was everything is father. I wanted that. I wanted a little boy...a little Khian. No matter what happened to Khi, I was gonna be a good mother to our child and I was gonna make sure that it knew that their father was a great man. And I was gonna make sure that I made frequent visits to Khi so that he could see his child as often as he was allowed to. I would never do no shit like what Selena was doing. She was so childish for that shit. She was happy as long as he was making monthly visits down there where she was at, but the minute he asked if he could bring Kenya home to stay with him for a few days at a time, she always had some type of excuse. She was so fuckin' pitiful and I just prayed that whatever the amount of time that Khi had to serve wasn't long so that he could pursue visitation rights with his daughter.

After lying in bed for a few minutes thinking about everything, I ended dozing off only to wake up hours later with Skylarr asleep right next to me. I pulled the cover over her not even knowing when she had even got in bed with me. I tried my hardest not to move so much so that I wouldn't wake her while reaching for my phone that sat a few feet away on the nightstand. I looked down at the screen and saw a few messages from Emon.

Emon: This bitch tripping man. She done called my brother and told him that we slept together. Sent this nigga a screenshot of our conversation.

I shot up in bed and unlocked the screen to my phone and went to the messages between Emon and I, it had been a few hours since he had sent it to me. I started sweating and immediately got sick to my stomach. I ran to the bathroom and pushed the toilet seat up with force. Everything that I had to eat the night before came up fast and hard. I coughed and tried to catch my breath as more vomit came out of my mouth. Tears stung my eyes as I thought back to the text message that I got from Emon. How the fuck did his girlfriend get his phone and why would she send that shit to Khi; I thought to myself as I stood to my feet and wiped my mouth with the back of my hand. My focus came up to the mirror and what I saw staring behind me scared the fuck out of me.

Khi.

14

KHI

"Hi, Papi, this is Yas, your sister-in-law. Look I think that you should you know that my boyfriend and Emon are fucking each other. Take a look at these messages I'm about to send you. I wasn't gonna say anything, but this is the second time that I have caught them sending each other inappropriate messages and since Emon wants to cheat on me, I'm telling you. You...okay...bye," Yasline's voice blasted through the speaker of my phone as I stood behind Cuba raging with so much anger. I had gotten a text right before I ran out of here a few hours ago from Tae saying that it was show time. He had finally gotten the names of the niggas that had ratted me out. He had already heard that they were in Houston so that was where I was already about to head, but when that text came through, I ran out of here ready. This damn jail sentence had been hanging over my head like a muthafuckin' sickness. I was doing and preparing shit like I would never walk the face again. I guess in the back of mind, I knew that once I stepped foot inside of that cell, I would be dead to everyone. Everybody would move on with their lives and the muthafuckin' streets would forget all about me. Cuba claimed that she would hold me down, but part of me knew that as much as she ran from me in the past, she was sure about to run away from this shit. That was if I didn't kill her muthafuckin' ass first.

"Kh—" Cuba tried to get out, but I wrapped my hand around her throat and squeezed until I saw slob coming out the side of her mouth. I held on to her long enough to make feel like her life was dangling right before her. Soon as I saw her eyes roll behind her head, I let her go and watched as she scratched at her throat and gasped for her. I slid my hands into my pocket, confused, hurt, and mad as a muthafucka.

At first, when Yasline called my phone, I thought that she was bugging. Emon had already told me she was a nutty ass bitch just like Selena so I paid her as no never mind until them muthafuckin' screenshots came through my line. I was headed to Houston ready to claim my muthafuckin' freedom when I turned around in the middle of the fuckin' freeway and hit 120 all the way back to the crib for this shit. Both Cuba and Emon had me fucked up.

"You grimy ass bitch! You did some hoe ass shit like that then got the nerve to be in my muthafuckin' crying and complaining about me fuckin' my baby mama one time! You dirty ass bitch!" I roared becoming angrier by the second. The more Cuba stood in front of me helpless and crying acting like she was in so much pain, further pissed me off. Thinking about all the months I begged this bitch to forgive me for the shit I had done. Had me going crazy in these muthafuckin' streets over not having her to come home to. Being reckless as a muthafucka and snapping on any and everybody. Turned me into a low-key muthafuckin' drug addict because she wanted to be a fuckin' bitch and play a nigga with that cat and mouse shit cause she knew I was down for the chase all for me to find out in the end that she fucked my punk ass little brother. These days before having to turn myself in had me wondering if it was because of her that I had got caught up and allowed these bitch ass niggas to see my face one day, hear my voice, or incidentally told my name to the wrong muthafucka. The way I had gotten caught up with this shit was crazy and I still couldn't piece any of it together.

I turned my head for a slight second to lean up against the wall in the bathroom when I was knocked over the head and damn near went stumbling to the ground. Next thing I know, I looked up to see Cuba had knocked me upside my shit with her big ass blow dryer. She had dropped the shit was coming at me with a pair of scissors. I backed away from her little ass and sucked my teeth when she swung at me and nicked me cross my arm. I looked down and saw the blood then looked up to see her crazy ass was still coming for me.

"Get the fuck back!" I yelled and continued to back up away from her until I was in the bedroom. When she swung at me again, I grabbed her by her arms and threw her on the bed. I brought her hand up to slap the fuck out of her, when I was pulled back and punched in my damn jaw.

"Get the hell off of her nigga!" Emon yelled and I heated with anger. I hopped up on my feet so fast and charged at that nigga like he wasn't even my flesh and blood. I hit that nigga with hook after hook, drawing blood with every punch. He fell back onto the ground and pounced on him, pounding his muthafuckin' face in. I told this little that I was gonna make him use his hands if he kept fucking with me. He tried it though, but Emon knew he wasn't a match for me.

I brought my fist up once again ready to black this nigga out when a muthafuckin' shot rang out behind me. I rolled off Emon and held onto my damn ear because of how close the shit seemed. When I looked up, Cuba stood there pointing one of my many pistols at me and looking like one of them deranged bitches off an episode of Snapped. Her hair was all over her head and she had slob or some shit caked up on the side of her mouth.

"Get off of him and leave, Khi, before you make me fuckin' shoot you! Don't you ever put your got damn hands on me nigga!" Cuba said shoving the gun forward and causing the muthafuckin' trigger fire a bullet right next to my damn head.

"Damn this what we come to? You gonna kill me behind my little brother! How long y'all been fuckin around, Cuba?" I said and crawled backwards on the floor. I watched as tears poured from Cuba's eyes as she kept the damn gun pointed towards me.

"I should kill your ass for putting your damn hands on me! The last nigga that put his hands on me fuckin' raped me, you wanna rape me too, Khil?" Cuba yelled and once again she shoved that gun in my direction with every word that she spoke. I slowly got up from the floor and then backed away towards the door.

"You and this nigga made to be together. What kinda shit y'all got going on? Trusted your wack ass, fucking' married you and you wanna turn around and marry my fuckin brother. It was other badder bitches that I could've wifed and this how you do a nigga, Cuba."

"Fuck him, Cuba. Let that nigga go," Emon said from the floor and that shit pissed me off. I took me feet and kicked that nigga in his stomach when Cuba charged at me. Next thing I knew, we were wrestling over the gun and I never knew she had so much damn strength. It took everything I had to take the damn hammer from her ass and as soon as I did, it went off, a bullet from the chamber slamming right into my right into my little brother's stomach.

My muthafuckin' heart stopped immediately as I watched Emon grab at his gut and start to gasp for air. I dropped the piece and quickly ran over to him. Pulling my shirt off my back, I balled it up and stuffed it into his wound trying to stop all the blood that poured out of him.

"Cuba, call an ambulance. Ahh, fuck! Emon, shit my nigga. I ain't mean to do that shit," I said and watched as a tear fell from my eye and onto his face.

Emon reached down to touch his stomach and then brought his fingers up to his face to look at them. He looked from Cuba and then to me and I watched as his face was suddenly covered with agony. He opened his mouth to speak, but only gargling sounds came out.

I could hear Cuba behind me on the phone with the ambulance and silently prayed to myself that they would get here fast. I was mad, but I wasn't that damn mad at the little nigga. I would never wish death on the kid for nothing ever. I had a hand raising this little nigga and he was a like damn son to me. I taught his ass how to tie his fuckin' shoes, how to aim his damn dick so he could stop pissing all over the wall and floor as a little nigga. I used to help him and Dae both with their homework and taught both of them niggas the proper way to wear a damn condom. When they was old enough, I showed them how to cook crack and the right way on how to tote and use a pistol. I took care of my brothers and I loved them, which was why I knew I had to do whatever I had to do to either stay out of jail or make my sentence as short as possible.

"I...I...didn't want to. He made me...," Emon said before his lips trembled and looked off to the left of him. I grabbed his hand into mine and looked down at him.

"Don't say nothing. Just squeeze my hand and keep breathing," I told him and I could feel Cuba standing closely behind me. I looked up at her with so much hate in my eyes and knew that if my brother didn't make it, I would forever blame her for it.

"I'm sorry! I should've said something, but...we..."

"No...no..." Emon protested and Cuba backed away and started crying. I looked from him and then to her and then back at Emon. Tears started gathering in my eyes noticing how much weaker he was getting.

"Did you call them? How long did they say?" I yelled to Cuba as she paced back and forth across the bedroom floor.

"They on their way," Cuba cried.

"I ain't mad at you bruh." I said to Emon causing Cuba to scoff behind me.

"You ain't got no reason to be at him! He did what he was forced to do...not what he wanted to do!" Cuba yelled and I looked back at her with a confused look on my face.

"Fuck is you talking about?" I asked her and she mumbled a few words before she just started yelling some shit that sent me silent.

"Why couldn't you just leave it alone, Khi? Damn it," Cuba cried behind me and I couldn't help but let out a cry myself. I looked down at my brother and kissed him on the forehead. No longer wanting to wait on the ambulance, I pulled Emon into my arms and carried him out of my bedroom and down the stairs. Soon as I made it outside of the house and down the steps that led to my drive-way, I could hear the sirens blaring in the distance.

I signaled for one of the goonies guarding the gate to open it and met the Ambulance halfway. They came to a stop and hopped out and took Emon from me. He was still breathing, but I didn't know for how long. Once they strapped him down to the gurney and placed him on the back of the bus, I climbed inside with them and watched as they went to work trying to save my little brother's life.

Fuck; I thought to myself thinking about the words that Cuba said to me.

I didn't have sex with Emon. I tried to run from Chaison when he tried to rape me again and because of it, he struck me across my back with a chain and then forced Emon to do it. He made Emon have sex with me.

15
CUBA

2 ½ months later...

"Your honor, we have evidence to show that the government's own Destiny Davis-Henson planted evidence against my client and the DNA that was found on Jourdin Lewis' body was placed there doing the time she was in the morgue," KaeDee said and I looked around the court room and my eyes landed on Destiny', KaeDee's former girlfriend and baby mama. She stood to her feet and placed her hand over her small, but round belly before rushing out of the courtroom.

Me an Tangie looked at each other and I grabbed her hand and squeezed it for reassurance. Cassidy had been on house arrest for almost three months waiting for this very day and Tangie had been on pins and needles waiting to see what the outcome of this day would be.

Her and Cass were no longer together, but still living in the same house since Cass had used their address as the place he would be residing until his trial date. Cass had called off the engagement a few weeks after Khi had turned himself in telling Tangie that he felt like they were better off as friends.

At first Tangie was hurt and spent most of the days afterwards locked up in the bathroom crying when she had a free moment, but I guess she started to realize that maybe Cassidy was right. They had more miserable moments together than they had apart. As friends, they laughed more and got along way better. I saw the change in Cassidy immediately when he no longer had the pressure of making Tangie happy on his shoulders. My cousin was hard on Cass and she had every right to be, but I agreed with Cassidy on certain situations.

No matter how many times Tangie said she forgave Cass for his wrongdoings, she still allowed his actions to eat at her and could never allow herself to be happy with him. She would always find blame in something that he did and rode him hard as hell about it until she felt like he'd had enough. I had learned from their relationship to not harbor on mistakes and it was either you forgave and let go, or you just let go.

"Not only do we believe that Agent Davis Henson has tampered with evidence in the case of the State V Prince, we also have proof to show that this government official has tampered with witnesses in the government's case versus Khian Prince. Yes, your honor before the prosecution steps in to say anything about my relationship with Davis Henson, I had no idea what was happening until after it happened. It seems that Henson has a long history of planting evidence and altering cases to get the conviction that she's want. I have text messages, voicemails of plenty of arguments between the two of us of how she used my brothers to get back at me for our breakup," KaeDee said and I shook my head. I knew that something wasn't right with everything that was going on. The reason that the FEDs were coming after Khi didn't seem right. The shit was strange and I knew that there was no way Khi would make that big of a mistake and put himself in a position for niggas to take him away from his family.

All this shit was all behind the chick that he had been warning KaeDee about from the very beginning. I was glad to see that KaeDee didn't have no qualms about ratting her ass out and putting his brother before her. It was only right. He had neglected them in their time of need all because of Destiny and to see him doing his all to make up for it said a lot. She was pregnant with his baby, and after this, she would more than likely spend the rest of her pregnancy behind bars and then lose her child. I know it had to hurt KaeDee to do this to her, but it was time that the bitch played with the cards she had dealt to herself.

"With that evidence that has been presented to the court, we have no choice but to dismiss the case and all charges against Cassidy Prince are to be dropped immediately," the judge said and banged his gavel. He stood up from his chair and Tangie and I hugged each other and rushed out of the courtroom to wait for Cass to come out. Now that Cass was free from the charges that he was facing, I knew there was only a matter of time before Khi would be free as well.

My baby had been gone away from me for two months and every day I hated myself for all the shit that I put him through. I wished that all that time I spent running from him was time that I had spent loving him instead. It seemed like being that I had spent time in jail myself that I should've known how quickly things could turn around and person could be snatched away and locked away for years and years. In this case, I took advantage and instead of allowing Khi to love me, I allowed the hurt that another nigga caused to me to block the blessing that God had for me.

I was hopeful that as easy as this was for Cass that it would be the same for Khi. I was due to have our first child together in September and all I could was pray that he would be able to be a part of it.

"Hey, Emon," I said to him when he walked out of the courtroom holding hands with his new girlfriend Khloe. She was a better fit for him than the last chick that he was with. The crazy ass bitch that caused all that madness that led to Khi damn near killing his little brother. After that day, Emon spent six hours fighting for his life on a surgery table. The doctors saved him thankfully, but he had lost so much blood that he ended up slipping into a coma for a little over a month.

He had just gotten home and had met Khloe at the rehabilitation center he had been attending while getting therapy. Since being shot, he had issues with his leg and she was one of the nurses that helped him gain his strength back. She was a pretty looking girl, but I couldn't help but think that she looked a little too straight to handle Emon. He was a savage just like his brothers and always too eager to get into some shit. Him and Dae had been hanging real tough since he'd been out of prison and now that Dae didn't have a woman that he was trying to prove his changed ways too, he was sort of back to his reckless ass ways. It was only a rumor, but I had heard that Dae and Emon had gone to Houston and had slumped a few niggas that were believed to be the ones snitching on Khi. Even then the FEDs had still held on to my baby saying that the witness were not needed to convict Khi. So hopefully now that KaeDee had proved that the basis of their evidence more than likely came from a crooked agent, they would drop everything and free him.

"What's up, sis? How everything been?" Emon asked me and I sighed and touched my little, round belly.

"I can't complain," I told him. "Just hoping we can get the same outcome for Khi."

Emon nodded agreeing with me before he pulled Khloe's hand to his mouth and kissed the back of it. Tangie told me that Cass let her know that he was getting counseling as well for what he had to do to me. He felt so bad and I knew that it was the reason why his relationship with Khi wasn't the same as it was before.

He tried to say it was for the fact that Khi didn't tell him that they didn't share the same father, but I always knew different. Emon and I both cried like little babies that day Chaison tortured the both of us from trying to get away from him. I was embarrassed and so was Emon. He felt like the sickest nigga in the world and felt like he was weak for not being able to fight Chaison off.

After it happened, Emon begged me not to tell Khi what happened cause he feared that Khi would never look at him the same. I promised Emon that I would never say anything because I also felt like Khi would look at me differently too.

Since he had been locked up, they allowed he and I to have face to face visits where we could really sit down and talk to one another and I had found out that a lot of nights he sat up crying about what happened. The guilt and being consumed by those walls had ate way at him and he had even grown a few gray hairs. It took a lot of me telling how much I loved him and I didn't blame him for what happened for him to finally get in a better place. He was dead set on pushing me away and telling me that I needed to find someone better to live my life with, but I knew that was just him feeling bad about shit and not the way he truly felt.

I would never leave his side in a time like this. I remembered how good I felt just having Tangie writing me and sending me books to read. She was a God send and had it not been for her, I would've never made it through. Khi was my husband and even though, I had run before, I couldn't dare run away from him now.

"A'ight, one down and one to go," KaeDee said as he emerged from the courtroom. He loosened his tie and I followed behind him while Tangie ran into Cass' arms. They hugged each other and I looked back to see him place a kiss on her forehead and then engage in conversation with her.

"Do you think this is going to work for Khi's case?" I asked KaeDee desperately.

"I don't know. I'm hopeful, but the FEDs are a whole other ball game. They can claim that they are holding Khi for reasons that have nothing to do with why they charged him the first place and it would be nothing that we could do about it."

"Oh wow, so it's possible that he might not be coming home," I asked becoming emotional.

"It's possible, but don't get too caught up in your feelings just yet baby girl. Let me get with my people today and I'll get with you. Stay calm. It's gonna be alright."

I nodded and allowed KaeDee to walk away and I headed to my car. Once I got inside, I laid my against the steering wheel and just prayed. At this point, it was all that I could do.

16

EPILOGUE

Khi

I sat across the table from KaeDee and his partners discussing a plea deal the government was trying to get me to take. Even after the bruh was able to prove that his bitch had set all this shit into motion, they were still trying to stick it to my ass. Now that they couldn't get me for drug charges, they were trying to get me for money laundering. I hadn't wanted to plead guilty to that, but after them niggas came through and seized all the shit that I had left in my name, it was the only way I as gonna be able to answer to how I was able to afford it all without them prying further into my life and then possibly fucking with my brothers too.

They had taken everything. All my cars, the house that I had just purchased for me, Cuba, and the kids. I had about a hundred and fifty thousand dollars in cash that I called myself hiding, but them bitches found that and took that too. I was thankful though cause they didn't find not one damn drug besides a couple of bags weed that I had laying around the house. Police ass niggas thought they was shutting shit down, but from my understanding and although it was scary as fuck, Dae and Emon had the shit on lock. Tamar wasn't too happy with it, but he couldn't too much complain. Shit his money was always on time and the streets wasn't complaining. The only thing that I guess he really wasn't cool with was the fact that Dae and Emon was too hot headed ass niggas and they had slumped a few niggas just to make statements that didn't even really need to be made. Prince—Prince Gang---Prince Boys, was forever written. They could get rid of one of us, but they never could get rid of us all. And as soon as they thought we were at our weakest, one of us stepped up and put all that shit to rest. They could never stop the kid kid for too long. I was gonna sit down and do this little time, but I promise then when I came home, the shit I was gonna do was gonna be shit that couldn't be stopped. Tamar had already promised me a seat at the table. Long as I didn't snitch of course, which was something that he most definitely didn't have to worry about. I wasn't no pussy ass nigga. I was gonna do this time and allow my mind to expand and breathe. Shit sometimes a nigga needed a little peace after running the streets damn near his whole life and if this was the only way that I could get it, then fuck it.

KaeDee was able to talk them down to me doing three years where I only had to serve about 80-85 percent of that. So in a good 2 years and a few months I was coming home. The only fucked up thing was that Cuba would be alone raising Skylarr and the kid she had on the way. If anything tore me up it was that and the fact that all that had transpired with Chaison, her, and my brother was fresh as fuck. The news of all that had really happened was still coming out piece by piece and I ain't know how shawty was dealing with it because the shit was killing me on the inside. Thinking about my wife and what she had gone through was the only thing that kept me up at night and half the time shedding tears. I didn't even know I could cry as much as I had, but I guess when you found real, true love, nothing could stop you from hurting when they were hurting.

Cuba claimed to be good, but you could never know with her. One minute she would be good and the next she would be bawling in tears. One thing I knew was that no matter what, she had an army of niggas looking out for her and making sure that her and the kid was good in my absence.

"A'ight, sign right here?" I asked and sighed. KaeDee nodded and I put my name on the line in the place where it asked for my signature and the date. It was crazy how the justice system worked. Shit wasn't designed to work out in a young black nigga's favor. No matter how much money a nigga had, they was doing anything they could think of to take it away. Black people wasn't supposed to prosper. Not even off to the shit that they had tossed in our neighborhoods to kill us. Black people got the most time for drug related crimes simply because it was created to tear us down and not bring us up. So if you ever called yourself making a dollar off that shit, best believe they was gonna make you pay with your life. I had been one of the lucky ones. Hell we all had, escaping excruciating drug charges and sentences by the skin of our teeth.

"It's done, sad to say that I will see you back on this side in a couple of years," KaeDee said and I nodded. I stood to my feet and we hugged for a long while and said our goodbyes before he and the pigs from the FEDs wrapped up their paperwork and then left me in the room alone. After a couple of minutes, Cuba and the kid came through the door. Skylarr ran into my arms and I picked her up and kissed all over her. She was dressed in a pretty pink dress with a bunch of ponytails and barrettes all over her head. I tickled her into a laughing fit before she was crying for me to put her down.

"I missed you," I told Skylarr and kneel down so that was closer to her height.

"Miss you," Skylarr said shyly and I chuckled and pulled her into a hug, squeezing her tight. I knew she was in good hands but it was making me sick to know I was going to miss the next couple of years of her life. She would start her first day of kindergarten while I was gone and more than likely lose her first tooth.

"You been good for your mama?" I asked choking up a little. Skylarr nodded and I kissed her again before I ran my hand over her face and told her how much I loved her.

"Come on baby, lets go back outside with your uncle," Cuba told her and tried to pick Skylarr up and I popped her hand and pulled her into my arms.

"Let her stay," I said to Cuba and kissed her cheek and then her lips. "Thank you baby."

"Thank me for what? What did I do?"

"Cause I never thought your little nappy headed, flat booty, ashy knee-cap having ass would have me falling in love and losing my damn mind behind it at that."

"Why you always gotta call me ashy? And nigga you know my weave been fresh lately so don't even front," Cuba said and we both chuckled.

"Yea, you been showing out, but I like when you ugly tho ma cause I know won't nobody want your ass but me."

"You so damn mean and it doesn't matter who wants me because all I want is you."

"You sure about that? Now is your time to run and this time I wouldn't even be mad at you. I understand."

"Understand that before I was afraid of love because I thought that I wasn't worth and scared that you would only hurt me and leave me in the end. But you've honestly showed me that I was and that I was deserving of unconditional love and deserving of a happy life. Although the road has been rocky for us and we still have bumps and humps to get over, I'm happy Khi. We have a beautiful daughter, another one on the way, and I'm hoping that I can establish some good communication with Selena and encourage her to come around for the sake of Kenya. We're gonna be fine. If I at any point felt like this was something that I couldn't do, then I would've told your ass. I feel stronger than ever now and knowing that you're depending on me makes me only wanna show how true of a rider I am. Don't worry baby, we gonna be good."

"Straight. Well long as I know you goof then I'm good."

"Don't even worry nigga. We gonna be right back down during visiting hours in two days and I'm gonna write you as soon as I get home. Khi, don't be worrying about me. I'm okay. I promise you I am," I told Khi and I noticed the tears that had gathered in his eyes and that only made me cry. Khi pulled me in for a hug and I rested my head into his chest. "I really am okay, Khi."

"Okay...a'ight. I'mma let you have that," I told Cuba and grabbed both sides of her face with my hands. I leaned over and kissed her lips and then stared into her eyes.

"You need to just believe me and relax."

"I'll relax when I walk out the other side in 2 ½ years. I love you, Cuba."

"I love you too, Khi."

The End.

CPSIA information can be obtained
at www.ICGtesting.com
Printed in the USA
LVHW021454080219
606907LV00017B/697/P